## "Of course. Bring the dog."

Randy had always liked dogs. His customers wouldn't mind. In fact, they'd probably linger in the store even more because of him. Maybe he'd get a dog of his own after he moved into the new house. It was a thought.

"Thanks." She came over and gave him a quick hug. "I'll open the store tomorrow at nine. You're closed on Sundays, right?"

"Right." He stood paralyzed from the shock of her touch as she hurried to the back. The sound of the screen door slamming jolted him out of his stupor.

Hannah almost made him forget he wasn't like any other guy.

And he wasn't.

He had a secret. And that secret would stay with him until the day he died.

When that day came, he'd be single.

He had to be more careful around Hannah Carr. There was something about her that made his logic go into hiding. He couldn't afford to forget he couldn't have her.

**Jill Kemerer** writes novels with love, humor and faith. Besides spoiling her mini dachshund and keeping up with her busy kids, Jill reads stacks of books, lives for her morning coffee and gushes over fluffy animals. She resides in Ohio with her husband and two children. Jill loves connecting with readers, so please visit her website, jillkemerer.com, or contact her at PO Box 2802, Whitehouse, OH 43571.

## Books by Jill Kemerer

### Love Inspired

#### *Wyoming Ranchers*

*The Prodigal's Holiday Hope*
*A Cowboy to Rely On*
*Guarding His Secret*

#### *Wyoming Sweethearts*

*Her Cowboy Till Christmas*
*The Cowboy's Secret*
*The Cowboy's Christmas Blessings*
*Hers for the Summer*

#### *Wyoming Cowboys*

*The Rancher's Mistletoe Bride*
*Reunited with the Bull Rider*
*Wyoming Christmas Quadruplets*
*His Wyoming Baby Blessing*

Visit the Author Profile page at LoveInspired.com for more titles.

# Guarding
# His Secret

## Jill Kemerer

**LOVE INSPIRED**
INSPIRATIONAL ROMANCE

# LOVE INSPIRED®
## INSPIRATIONAL ROMANCE

Recycling programs
for this product may
not exist in your area.

ISBN-13: 978-1-335-75929-0

Guarding His Secret

Copyright © 2022 by Ripple Effect Press, LLC

For questions and comments about the quality of this book, please contact us
at CustomerService@Harlequin.com.

Love Inspired
22 Adelaide St. West, 41st Floor
Toronto, Ontario M5H 4E3, Canada
www.LoveInspired.com

Printed in U.S.A.

Trust in the Lord with all thine heart;
and lean not unto thine own understanding.
In all thy ways acknowledge Him,
and He shall direct thy paths.
—*Proverbs* 3:5–6

This book is dedicated to my dear friend Barb Roose. You inspire me. You see the best in people. You make me believe anything is possible. I am thankful every day for your friendship. The world needs more women like you.

A special thank-you to Shana Asaro for giving me the opportunity to write about service dogs. What a treat! I appreciate all you do to help my career.

And for all you women out there who get things done—the Hannahs of the world—I salute you!

# Chapter One

"Wake up."

Randy Watkins rolled over and squinted at the overhead light in his eyes. What time was it? Had he slept late or something?

"I've got to take off." Austin, his older brother, hopped around on one foot as he tried to pull a sock on the other.

"Where are you going?" Randy rubbed his eyes and propped himself up on his elbows. He checked the time. A little past two in the morning. The intensity of Austin's movements set off alarm bells.

"I've got an emergency. I'll be in Texas for a week. Maybe two." His face could have been carved from granite. "You're in charge of the ranch. Bo left two days ago to visit his grandkids in Alabama. Won't be back for a month."

That woke him up.

Randy flung the blankets aside and got out of bed. Bo Nichol had been Austin's foreman on the ranch for over ten years. Between Bo and Austin, the cattle operation ran as smoothly as could be, leaving Randy free to pursue his own career.

Austin had wrangled the sock on and was headed down the hall. Randy followed him to his room, where Austin shoved a few shirts into a bulging duffel bag.

"What about the store?" Randy leaned against the doorframe.

"Find someone else to run it." Austin leveled him with the I'm-older-than-you-and-you'd-better-obey-me stare he'd perfected when they were kids. Except neither was a kid anymore. Just two grown men doing their best to live the way their father taught them.

The strain in his brother's expression chased away his natural inclination to argue. Whatever was going on was big, which meant Randy would have to find someone to run Watkins Outfitters, his bait and tackle shop in downtown Sunrise Bend, Wyoming. "I've got you covered, man."

Austin nodded.

"What's the emergency?" He doubted he'd get a straight answer. He knew his brother too well. It was one of the reasons Randy was moving out of the old family farmhouse as soon as the construction of his new house was finished. He was ready for his own space. At twenty-nine, he couldn't wait to live on his own.

"I can't say. I don't have all the information yet." Austin averted his gaze and visibly swallowed. "I know this is short notice. I wouldn't ask if it wasn't important."

"Well, technically, you didn't ask." He tried to lighten the mood. "You ordered."

Austin shot him a brief glare and resumed packing. Then he hoisted the duffel over his shoulder. "A week, Randy. Two, tops. Remember, we have an agreement."

Oh, he remembered, all right. They'd made promises to each other after Dad died. They'd agreed they would always have each other's back. Brothers first. No matter what.

Dad would have wanted it that way. Pneumonia had taken their mother when Randy was two. Their grandparents had passed away years ago. A few distant aunts and uncles had never been in their lives. Randy and Austin relied on each other and always would.

And since Austin's life revolved around the cattle, the ranch would be Randy's top priority until he returned.

"Don't worry about a thing. I'll take care of this place." He stepped aside to let him pass. They continued down the staircase to the kitchen. He wished his brother would have enough faith in him to tell him what was going on, though. "Whatever this is…you can trust me with it."

"I know." Austin's expression was bleak. "I'll tell you everything, but I have to evaluate the situation for myself first."

He understood. His brother was the opposite of rash. He thought things through before blabbing or acting. If he said it was an emergency and he had to get more info, he meant it. It had been years and years since Randy had seen him this traumatized.

"Want me to go with you?" he asked. "You're pretty rattled."

"No." Austin pulled on his cowboy boots. "Just take care of the cattle. I'll text you with the specific ones to keep an eye on."

As Austin turned to leave, Randy had the strongest urge to hug him. They weren't very affectionate with each other. Roughhousing was as physical as they got. But seeing his big brother this upset tugged at the little boy inside him, the one who loved and admired Austin more than anyone on earth.

Randy reached out, pulled him into a quick embrace and stepped back. Gratitude gleamed in Austin's eyes, then he raised his hand in goodbye and walked out the door.

When the sound of the truck engine faded, Randy debated his next move. There was no way he'd be able to get back to sleep now. The list of work he'd have to do in Austin's absence loomed like the Bighorn Mountains in the distance. The ranch had two part-time cowboys in addition to Bo. Maybe they would put in extra hours.

Even if they did, Randy needed to ride out and check the cattle, feed the horses and deal with the steers. At least he didn't have to feed the cattle, too. They were grazing in pastures for the summer. He'd probably need to move them around, though, and calves could be tricky to nudge in the right direction.

He'd never been great at ranching. It had been his dad's and Austin's passion and, he hated to admit it even to himself, their bond over the ranch had always made him feel like the odd man out.

After putting on a pot of coffee, he sat at the kitchen table. How was he going to take care of the ranch, run the store and finish the projects at his new house? To save money, he was painting the rooms, ordering the appliances, tackling the landscaping and doing other odd jobs. Most of it needed to be done before he moved in at the end of the month.

Maybe Finn could work extra hours at the store…

*Nope.* Randy tipped his head back and sighed. His sole employee was out of town for the next two weeks. Finn had graduated from high school on Saturday, and his parents were taking him on a trip to Florida to celebrate. Boy, did he need the kid now.

Blowing out a breath, he thought hard for a solution. Couldn't ask just anyone to watch the store, not during the busy season.

What if he asked Blaine to help with the cattle?

That wouldn't work. Blaine Mayer and his brother, Jet, had their hands full dividing their ranch. And with their sister's out-of-town wedding coming up next weekend, they were too busy to help. His other friend Mac Tolbert would pitch in if need be. But he, too, had his own cattle operation to run. And their buddy Sawyer Roth was planning his wedding to Tess Malone in addition to managing her ranch.

Randy had grown up with the guys. They'd do anything for him, the same way he'd do anything for them. But he wouldn't even consider pawning the ranch work off on them unless he couldn't find anyone to watch the store.

As the coffeemaker gurgled, he rose and leaned against the counter, weighing his options.

He didn't have time to train someone who had no experience, and he couldn't think of any locals who didn't already have a job. Watkins Outfitters was more than a bait and tackle shop. It went way beyond rods and worms. Camping and hunting equipment were popular year-round. He sold specialty products to outdoor enthusiasts, and right now everyone was eager to cast a line.

For the past two months, the new lures had been coming in, and he'd been creating videos every week to discuss the pros and cons of each. All of it took time and energy.

*Remember, we have an agreement.*

*Yeah, yeah, yeah.*

If his brother couldn't count on him in an emergency, then Randy might as well hang his head in shame and leave town. The ranch was everything to Austin, and he didn't want his brother worrying about it on top of everything else.

Whatever *everything else* entailed.

He poured himself a cup of coffee, held the steaming mug between his fingers and looked unseeing out the window at the darkness beyond.

Who could he get to help out at the store?

An image of long blond hair, blue eyes, a sunny smile and a sarcastic streak a mile wide came to mind.

Hannah.

Of course.

School had just let out for the summer. As a local third-grade teacher, she'd be free for a few months. She'd filled in for several local businesses before she'd been hired to teach full-time, so it wasn't as if he couldn't trust her with the store. She was smart, great with customers and, hopefully, available.

She was also the prettiest thing he'd seen around here since…well…ever. Until recently, he'd always thought of her as nothing more than a fun pal. But something had started changing. He kept noticing her big smile and equally big heart. It made him uncomfortable. So he tried not to be around her too much.

*Lord, if there's anyone else I can ask to help out, lead me to them.*

He sipped his coffee, searching his thoughts for any suitable person.

But his mind remained blank.

Sighing, he accepted the facts. He was in a bind, and Hannah was the ideal person to help him.

Too bad she was the last person in Sunrise Bend he wanted to ask.

\* \* \*

The next three months loomed before her bright with possibilities. Another successful school year had wrapped up. As much as Hannah Carr would miss the third-grade students she'd spent so much time with this year, she couldn't wait to begin her own adventures this summer.

She gripped a cardboard box overflowing with supplies. A small potted plant threatened to teeter off the top as she strolled toward the Sunrise Bend Elementary School parking lot. Late-afternoon sunshine warmed the bare skin of her arms. Number one on her agenda was to change out of this sundress and into comfy shorts and a tank top as soon as she got home. For the first Friday in June, it was unseasonably warm.

Thinking ahead to the weekend, she exhaled in contentment. No papers to grade, no lessons to plan. Plenty of time to clean her apartment and get ready for her new arrival.

In ten short days she was getting her first puppy! Well, not hers, exactly. She was finally becoming an official puppy raiser. She'd been volunteering for Paws at Your Service for over two years, teaching puppy training classes on Saturdays and helping the owner, Molly Dearborn, whenever possible. Molly had spent over two decades training and placing service dogs with a national organization before moving to Wyoming four years ago and opening her own business.

And now Hannah would have the opportunity to make a difference in someone's life by helping train a service dog. She'd seen firsthand how they helped people with disabilities. Jenna Delante, a fourth-grade student with cerebral palsy, had a golden retriever to help her balance, to open and shut doors and to retrieve items for her. The other students loved Duke, and Jenna was blossoming physically and socially with his help.

At the end of the sidewalk, Hannah turned, stepping onto the blacktop toward the staff parking lot. Part of her wished she could get the puppy today. She itched to get started training it before taking the little guy to school with her in the fall. She'd already gotten school board approval for the dog to be in her classroom. After fourteen months, she'd give the pup back to Paws at Your Service to advance its training—if it made the cut.

She'd make sure the puppy made the cut.

Firming her steps, she thrust her chin in the air. She'd succeed. She had to. There were so many people who desperately needed a service dog, and in some cases, they waited years for the opportunity.

Speaking of waiting lists…she'd also been on Molly's list to adopt a retired service dog for over eighteen months. She sighed. Maybe it was better she hadn't been placed with one yet. It would give her the opportunity to focus exclusively on the puppy.

Boy, this box was getting heavy. Her pace picked up when she spotted her red Jeep Wrangler in the nearly empty lot. She was definitely taking off the top panels today. Sun on her face, wind in her hair…

A familiar figure came into view. What was Randy doing here?

Even this far away she could make out his jeans and faded navy T-shirt as he leaned against the Jeep's driver's-side door, his profile to her as he stared out at the playground. Not overly tall nor bulgingly muscular, he fit together just right.

They'd been casual friends for years. She teased him like he was one of her brothers. He had hazel eyes, a straight nose, a strong chin and thin lips that smiled easily. His broad shoulders strained under the T-shirt, and his short, thick brown hair practically begged to be touched.

*Begged to be touched?*

The lack of sleep from the end of the school year must be messing with her head or something. She had no business thinking about touching Randy's hair. In fact, she shouldn't be thinking about him at all.

For years her mother had been pushing her to date one of the local cowboys, and Mom had a soft spot for Randy and his brother, Austin. It used to amuse Hannah. Now the relentless matchmaking efforts irritated her to the point that she wanted to scream she was never getting married, even if she secretly hoped to find a good man and have a couple of kids someday.

If she could find a guy who wanted the same things she did—love and commitment—she'd get married in a heartbeat. But so far, she hadn't found him.

She was so over men with lukewarm feelings. She'd rather be single forever than be someone's backup plan. None of the guys around here seemed in a hurry to get married, either, that was for sure. Well, except Sawyer, but he didn't count since he'd only recently moved back to Sunrise Bend and gotten engaged.

"Did you run out of fishing lures or something?" Hannah called out as she approached him.

He startled, turning to face her. *Huh.* She couldn't remember a time she'd caught Randy off guard. He always seemed to be two steps ahead of everything. Was something wrong?

"No. Still fully stocked." His lips curved up slightly.

"Here, let me help." He took the box from her, and her muscles cried out in relief.

She fished in her oversize purse for her keys. With a double chirp, the vehicle unlocked, and she went to the back to open the trunk. He set the box inside and shut the trunk. Then stood there. Inches from her. Causing the hair on her arms to rise.

"I'm sure you didn't come out here to help me move my plant." She backed away, cocking her head to the side, teasing him the way she always did. It chased away the unwelcome awareness of him.

"I have a favor to ask." His expression grew serious. Whatever the favor was, he was dealing with something major.

"What's going on?"

He looked around. So did she. Their only company was the blue sky and occasional bird flying overhead. Most of the other teachers had hightailed it out of there an hour ago.

"Austin took off in the middle of the night for an emergency."

"Oh no." She placed her hand over her chest. "Is everything okay?"

"I think so." Randy's eyebrows drew together as he diverted his attention to his feet. Then he looked up under dark lashes. "I'm in charge of the ranch for the next week or two. Puts me in a bind."

He didn't have to fill in the blanks. She could see his dilemma clearly. "You can't take care of the ranch and be at the store. Bo's on vacation, isn't he?"

"Yeah, he went down south to visit his family. Been planning it for over a year. He and Austin worked it out so he could take the month off."

Mom had raved on more than one occasion about how nice it would be for Bo to see his grandkids. Her mother seemed to know everything going on around here. "Do you need me to watch the store for you?"

He blinked, and the honesty, relief and appreciation in his expression surprised her. "Would you?"

"Yeah, of course." She waved as if it were nothing. "A week or two? I can do that." Then she remembered the puppy. "Oh, wait."

"What's wrong? You're busy, aren't you?" His shoulders dropped, and she couldn't help wanting to cheer him up.

"Well, kind of. It might not be a problem, though." She mentally worked through the situation. "I volunteered to be a puppy raiser for Paws at Your Service. I pick mine up not this Sunday but the next. If Austin isn't back... well...I'll help out until I get the puppy."

"I can ask Blaine or Mac to assist at the ranch if Austin's not back by then."

"And I could always ask my parents to take care of the puppy if need be." She didn't want to leave the dog with her parents unless absolutely necessary, though. Those early weeks were important for socialization and basic skills. She already had her daily training plan printed out. If she wanted to give the puppy the best chance at becoming a service dog, she needed to start off right.

"Or you could bring him to the store. I don't care." He smiled. "Whatever it takes."

A puppy in the store for hours would be a bad idea.

He rocked back on his heels. "I warn you now Joe Schlock will be talking your ear off for a couple of hours each day."

A breeze teased the hair around her neck. "Joe's a sweetheart."

"He's a seventy-nine-year-old pain in my side." He grinned. "But he's a good guy."

Hannah studied him briefly. This was the Randy she was familiar with. Easy smile, diplomatic, nice to everyone, a hard worker. But under it all she sensed there was more—much more—to him.

A mystery. Maybe that was why she'd been getting prickly when Mom baked cookies for him and Austin and asked her to drop them off.

Mysterious men weren't good for her. Because whatever she didn't know about them, she filled in with her own imagination. She'd mentally built up a guy or two to be the man of her dreams and been crushed when they didn't live up to her expectations.

She wouldn't do it again. Especially not after Shawn.

Randy shifted his weight from one foot to the other. "I know it's short notice, but could you start tomorrow?"

"Short notice? Try borderline no notice." She raised an eyebrow in mock indignation, glad to think about anything other than her ex. "When are you planning on showing me the ropes?"

"How about right now?"

"How about you let me change into some shorts?"

"How about you change and meet me at the store?" With a gleam in his eye, he hitched his chin to her. "I'll take you out for burgers afterward."

"What if I want a steak?"

"Hannah, I'll buy you a lobster, steak and anything else your heart desires if you'll help me out."

Anything her heart desired? Dangerous words for a recovering romantic. "Promise?"

"Promise." All the teasing drained from his face, leaving something bleak in its wake.

"Hey, don't worry." She playfully jabbed his arm. "I'm not taking you up on it. I won't break your wallet."

He shook his head slightly. "Break it all you want. I appreciate you helping me out."

This conversation felt way too heavy.

"Hey, put those muscles to use, will you? Help me get these roof panels off."

He let out a light snort. "No problem."

A few minutes later, she settled into the driver's seat with the blue sky above her. Randy waved to her, and she waved back. "See you at the store in a little bit."

He nodded, and she drove away.

She hoped Austin's emergency wasn't too serious. And she really hoped he'd be back within the week. She'd purposely requested a puppy from this litter so she'd have the entire summer to get the dog potty-trained and up to speed with basic obedience. It wouldn't be ideal to spend her first days in a situation where the puppy wouldn't get her full attention.

She couldn't risk a frisky dog underfoot at Randy's store. What if it affected the pup negatively? And then the little guy didn't make the cut for advanced training? All because she messed up in week one?

She pressed on the accelerator. She wasn't messing up because she'd already drawn the line. She'd help until the puppy arrived. After that, Randy was on his own.

Asking Hannah to run the store was the dumbest thing he'd done in a long time. And Randy had done his share of stupid. Like taking the polar plunge last January, or agreeing to hunt sandhill cranes on the hottest day on record with Blaine two years ago—never again. But this? This might surpass them all.

"Knock, knock," Hannah called through the open screen of the store's back door fifteen minutes later. That was quick.

"It's open." He waited for her to join him. Ten minutes, tops. That was all it would take to show her the basics. Then he'd be free to run over to the new house and knock off an item on his to-do list.

*Nope.* He smacked his forehead. He'd promised her food.

Another idiotic move on his part. He needed to keep his interaction with her as short and to the point as possible.

Because from the minute he saw all of her blond hair glinting in the sunlight in the school parking lot, he'd known he was making a big mistake. For whatever reason, Hannah Carr affected him. He was too aware of her. And it irritated him. He wasn't one to be aware of the single women around here. It wasn't as if he could act on any attraction.

This was all Austin's fault.

How in the world was Randy supposed to concentrate on speed training her with the trail of her fresh-smelling perfume lingering in the air? This was an outdoor outfitter shop. A place for hunters and fishing enthusiasts. A place smelling of earth and worms and rubber waders. Not coconut and flowers and all things female.

"I see you moved the camo next to the camping supplies. Smart." She checked the tag of an orange vest. Against his better judgment, he snuck a peek at her slim figure. Short-sleeved shirt, shorts and slip-on sandals with red toenail polish peeking out. The outfit was nothing out of the ordinary, but on her? He almost knocked over the box of lures he'd abandoned earlier.

"Yeah. I figured they went better together." He steadied the box, sneaking another peek her way.

She visited the store regularly, always on the hunt for the perfect gift for one of her brothers or her dad. Her oldest brother, David, was a general practitioner in town, and her other brother, Michael, ran their father's ranch. Both of them were married with children. Randy liked the Carrs, especially Hannah's mom, who treated him and Austin like they were family. Always sending homemade cookies and cakes their way, Miss Patty was a phenomenal cook.

"What do I need to know?" She faced him then, her big blue eyes full of expectation. He liked that about her. She didn't hide anything.

Well, everyone hid something. He'd certainly been hiding something for years—from this town, from his friends, even from his brother.

So what? It was nobody's business.

"Let's start with the basics." He gave her the quick tour of the displays, which she was already familiar with, then led her behind the counter to show her his checkout system. He took the stool, and she looked over his shoulder. Her presence was making his pulse race. He didn't like it or the reason why it was happening.

Standing, he gestured to the stool. "Here, why don't we switch places, so you can get the hang of it."

"Okay." She shrugged, smiling, and took his spot. Leaning over her shoulder wasn't much better. They were too close. He sprinted through the instructions as she jotted notes on a tiny notepad, flipping pages over as fast as she could fill them.

"What about deliveries?" She looked back at him.

"Don't worry about them," he said gruffly. "I'll be here every afternoon." He figured between him and the other cowboys, the ranch chores would be wrapped up by three o'clock each day. He'd drive straight here to relieve her. "If you can open at nine, I'll take over around three or four. I'll speed over as soon as I finish up at the ranch."

"Well, don't get yourself in an accident," she teased. "I can handle this, you know."

"I know."

He did know. Hannah was nothing if not capable.

But he seriously doubted he could handle being around her much. All this female energy in the store was going to be a problem. Because she tempted him to want things he couldn't have. And up until recently, he hadn't even wanted them.

Hannah's cell phone rang. "Do you mind if I take this?"

"Go ahead." He backed up to give her privacy, busying himself with a box of nets, but he could hear every word she said.

"You're kidding," she said breathlessly. "That's great news. Yes…Right now? I'd love to…You're serious? I can't believe it…"

Finally, she ended the conversation and turned to him with shining eyes. "I'm going to have to bail on the burgers."

"Oh?" Disappointment hit him hard. Did she have a date or something? She'd sounded excited on the phone.

"That was Molly. She has a dog for me."

"Another puppy?" He placed the box on the counter.

"No, a retired service dog." She looked ready to float through the air. "I've been on the adoption list forever.

The ones that have become available all went to either their original puppy raiser or someone higher on the list."

"Won't the dog be old?" Why would she want someone's ancient dog that might not live long?

"Some of them are. This one is eight. Too old to be placed for service, but he's still got a lot of good years left."

Something told him that even if the dog only had a couple of good months left, Hannah would be equally enthusiastic.

"I'm going to go pick him up." She lightly clapped her hands in happiness, and he kind of wished he could go with her.

"Let me get you the store key, then."

"Oh, wait." She winced. "I didn't think this through. Is there any way I can bring him with me to the store? He passed all of his obedience classes years ago. I'm sure he wouldn't cause any trouble. I just can't imagine bringing him home and then leaving him by himself all day before he has a chance to get to know me. He's used to being with someone all the time."

"Of course. Bring him." He'd always liked dogs. His customers wouldn't mind. In fact, they'd probably linger in the store even more because of him. Maybe he'd get a dog of his own after he moved into the new house. It was a thought.

"Thanks." She came over and gave him a quick hug. "I'll open the store tomorrow at nine. You're closed on Sundays, right?"

"Right." He stood paralyzed from the shock of her touch as she hurried to the back. The sound of the screen door slamming jolted him out of his stupor.

Hannah almost made him forget he wasn't like any other guy.

And he wasn't.

He had a secret. And that secret would stay with him until the day he died.

When that day came, he'd be single.

He had to be more careful around Hannah Carr. There was something about her that made his logic disappear like the morning dew. He couldn't afford to forget he couldn't have her. Couldn't have any woman, when it came down to it.

Austin had better get home soon.

# Chapter Two

With her heartbeat racing, Hannah entered the enormous pole barn on Molly Dearborn's property twenty miles south of Sunrise Bend. She'd walked through this door countless times over the past two years, but this was the first time she'd be leaving with a dog of her own. The circumstances were less than ideal, though, picking him up the night before she was working at Randy's store. Plus, it would mean the dog would have to adjust to life with her *and* a puppy in just a matter of days.

Was she up to the task of giving this dog a loving home while training the puppy? All her printed training plans mocked her.

She raised her chin. She'd figure it out.

The fluorescent lights and smells of disinfectant, kibble and dog fur always made her smile. Dogs. She loved 'em.

The training facility was bare bones and clean. Beyond the entrance, offices lined the right wall. The main training area was up ahead. A sea of blue rubber floor was sectioned off from the green turf in the rear of the building. Folding chairs were placed along the wall for people who brought their dogs to obedience classes. Several full-grown dogs were playing on the turf as one of the volunteers watched over them. An occasional *woof* filled the air.

"In here, Hannah."

She followed the voice to Molly's office. A desk topped with stacks of files, a set of bookshelves filled with books and binders, two chairs for guests and three empty dog beds rounded out the room. Molly sat behind the desk, typing on her old PC. Her dark brown hair was streaked with gray and pulled back in a frizzy ponytail. She wore large glasses, jeans and her signature royal blue sweatshirt with the Paws at Your Service logo.

Molly looked up and smiled. "You've been waiting a long time for this."

"I know." She rubbed her palms together. "Where is he?"

"Sit a minute first." She gestured to the chair with a flick of her wrist. "Let's talk about his history before you meet him and your brain turns to mush."

It was true. She wouldn't be able to focus on a thing that was said after she met the dog.

Molly clasped her hands and set them on the desktop, making sure she had Hannah's attention before speaking. "Ned spent sixteen months with a puppy raiser before I worked with him at my old job. He's a black Lab, mellow and smart. He's trained to detect and alert for a number of medical issues."

Ned. What a cute name! "Like what?"

"Low blood sugar, seizures, drops in blood pressure, fainting, that sort of thing. The man he was placed with died from a stroke last week, and a friend took Ned in until the family could make decisions. As I mentioned on the phone, Ned is too old to be placed with another patient, but he's healthy and doesn't show any signs of slowing down. His puppy raiser doesn't want to adopt at this time, and you're at the top of the list."

"I'm so excited." Although she yearned to meet Ned, first Hannah wanted a complete picture of the special dog she'd be bringing home. "Tell me more about his skills—how he alerts."

"Ned is very perceptive to changes in blood pressure as well as the scents caused by low blood sugar. He gets close to his owner when he first senses something being off, and his response escalates depending on the severity of symptoms. Nudging, licking, possibly mouthing the person's hand."

"Was he with his owner when the man died?"

"Yes. Ned might need some extra care and attention for a while, and that's why I'm so happy he'll be moving in with you. Now that you're on summer break, I think you two are going to be a perfect match."

Hannah tucked away the kind words, but worry pinched at her. "I had a situation come up. I'm going to be helping at my friend's store for a week or so. It's a bait and tackle shop. I plan on taking Ned with me. Do you think it will be too much for him? And do you have any concerns with me getting the puppy so soon after bringing him home?"

"He's been trained to be comfortable in all kinds of situations. He'll probably enjoy being in the store. And I think Ned might model the behavior your pup needs. Like I always say, the more experiences with other people, other animals and other places the puppy has, the better prepared it will be. But keep the puppy's interactions with dogs other than Ned to a minimum for the first month or so."

"No problem," Hannah said, relieved. Practical mat-ters crowded into her head. "Obviously, I have nothing prepared. No food, no crate, not even a leash."

"I've got you covered." Molly stood and came around the desk. "You can bring my gear back when you get your own. Now, are you ready to meet your dog?"

"Yes!"

"Well, come on." Molly led the way out of the office. They skirted the main training area on their way to the turf where dogs either played or relaxed.

Which one was he?

Molly called Ned's name, and a black dog stood and trotted over to her. "Good boy."

Hannah looked into Ned's big brown eyes and her heart did indeed turn to mush.

This was her dog. This sweet guy with his tongue lolling and a smattering of white hairs on his black head. She got teared up.

"Hi, Ned." She choked back her emotions as he sniffed her hand, then she scratched behind his ears as he sat looking up at her with those soulful brown eyes. "You're a good boy, aren't you?"

He seemed sad. Probably missed his owner. Poor thing.

"You brought joy to someone else's life." Hannah stroked his fur. "Now it's my turn to bring a little joy to yours."

She got to know him more and talked to Molly for a while longer before they loaded the crate, some dog food and a few toys into the Jeep. Then she opened the back door for Ned to get in. He hopped up to the back seat easily. After starting the vehicle, she looked back to make sure he was okay. He seemed relaxed.

"Well, Ned, this is the official start to our life together. I hope you learn to love me as much as I already love you."

She pulled out of the parking lot and reflected on everything that had happened today. The end of the school year. Randy needing her help. And getting the call about Ned.

The wind blew her hair as she turned toward Sunrise Bend.

Randy. She'd been all too aware of his toned arms, his patience while explaining the cash register and the faint scent of his bodywash—or was it cologne?

She could not afford to start viewing Randy as anything other than a friend. He certainly didn't think of her that way. And she didn't want him to. It would send her on another misguided path, one she'd told herself she wasn't going down again.

She'd pour her energy into pampering the dear dog who'd devoted his life to helping his previous owner. She couldn't wait to give Ned the life he deserved.


Were Mondays always this busy at Randy's store?

Hannah finished ringing out Joe Schlock, who'd followed her around the displays for over an hour, chatting about anything and everything. He was her final customer, and she hoped nobody else would come in. She was more than ready for some quality time with Ned. After two full days with the dog, she couldn't say they'd bonded. Maybe it just took time.

Ever since the town had caught wind of her working here on Saturday, she'd dealt with a nonstop line of people waiting at the counter. Some needed supplies. Others wanted to gossip. All were curious to know why she was there and Randy wasn't. She'd been careful not to mention to anyone the reason she was helping him out. In this town, news spread like lice at a sleepover.

Of course, Ned was part of the attraction, too. Everyone seemed to love her sweet dog. For his part, Ned was taking it all in stride. He was a good boy. Kept out of the way. Obeyed every command. Didn't let out a peep.

She felt bad keeping him stuck inside here all day, though. As soon as Randy relieved her, she was going to take him out for a nice long walk. But where? Her apartment complex didn't have much to offer beyond a few sidewalks. And she didn't feel like driving all the way out to her parents' ranch, although Dad had been smitten with Ned yesterday when she'd stopped by. The feeling had seemed to be mutual.

At this point, she got the impression Ned could take her or leave her. Kind of like most guys.

She must be tired if she was comparing Ned to her exes.

"We'll grow into our bond." She bent to pet him. "It takes time."

He blinked those melancholy eyes and didn't move.

The back door banged, and she and Ned both turned to look in that direction.

Randy flew inside looking as flustered as she'd ever seen him. "Sorry I'm late."

She gave him a once-over. "Are you all right?"

"What? Oh, yeah. Fine. Why?" Red-faced and out of breath, he bent to check the labels of the boxes he'd stacked behind the counter. He held two fingers to the pulse in his neck. Ned walked over, sat close to Randy and watched him.

"You seem…not yourself," Hannah said.

"No?" He avoided eye contact with her as Ned licked the back of his hand. "Just in a rush. I have a lot on my mind. Well, hey, there, boy." He smiled at the dog, and it almost took her breath away. It reminded her of when Randy was younger. She hadn't seen his carefree expression in years. Maybe he had more going on than she realized. He scratched behind Ned's ears. "How are you doing?"

"He's been a trouper." The proud-mama sensation spread through her chest as the dog's tail thumped while Randy loved on him.

He gave him a final pat. "I meant to get here earlier, but a stupid calf—" He shook his head. "Doesn't matter. I'll finish up. You can go."

"I can stick around a minute." She regarded him thoughtfully. He seemed so off, so agitated, so unlike himself. "Is it just the calf that has you bothered?"

"The calf, her dingbat mama, the installation of the kitchen cabinets being delayed. All of it. I have a lot of projects to finish at the house before I move in. Everything's kind of hitting me at once."

"The new place is out on Owl Creek Road, right? I haven't been out that way in a while. When can you move in?" She'd driven past Randy's secluded property a few months ago. It was less than a five-minute drive from town. A stream ran through the back of it, ideal for fly-fishing. She wasn't surprised an outdoorsman like him had decided to build there.

"The end of the month, if all goes well. I'm behind on my end." All the pink in his face lingered as he pulled the binder marked Orders from a shelf under the register and began flipping through it. Ned licked his hand again. He chuckled. "I like you, too, boy."

"What all do you have left to do?" she asked.

"Here or the house?" He frowned.

"Both." She went to the supply closet and grabbed a roll of paper towels and glass cleaner. Then she sprayed the counter and wiped it clean, keeping an eye on Randy the entire time. It didn't escape her notice that Ned was far more interested in him than her.

She supposed the dog might be more comfortable with men. After all, his previous owner had been one.

"I just need to check the orders. Then I've got to start painting the house tonight."

She tossed the dirty paper towels in the trash. Randy seemed more himself, and Ned had reclaimed his spot from earlier. She put the cleaning supplies away and grabbed her purse.

Randy accidentally bumped into her, and she let out an *oof.*

"Sorry." He whirled to face her. "Wasn't paying attention."

"No biggie." Randy's new house was only minutes away. Ned would probably love a walk around his property. Wildlife to sniff, a wide-open space for her to toss him his ball. "This is going to sound weird, but would you mind if I took Ned to your new place? I think he'd enjoy exploring your yard. I hate to coop him up in my apartment when he's been so good here all day. We'll be long gone by the time you get there."

"Oh, yeah, take him there. He'll love it." The corner of his mouth lifted. Then he stared at her with such intensity she almost fidgeted. "Want to tour the house? That is if you don't have plans and don't mind waiting for me to finish up here?"

Did she want to tour his house? Yes. A big yes. "You don't mind?"

"I take any chance I can to show it off."

"You're trying to rope me into painting with you, aren't you?" She winked, hoping she didn't appear too eager to check out his home. She was as nosy as her mother—she wouldn't deny it.

"Would I do that?" His teasing tone sent pleasant flutters to her tummy.

"Yes, you would. When do you think you'll be done here?"

"Would half an hour work?" he asked. "I planned on grabbing a pizza."

"I'll bring paper plates and napkins." She took Ned's leash. "See you over there."

"See ya."

Well, the day had just gotten interesting. Ned would get some fun outside time, and she would get to see Randy's house.

But a wee voice in her head warned her that spending more time with Randy was inviting trouble.

*Yeah, right.*

She was playing with her dog and having a slice of pizza, not walking down the aisle. It was time to lighten up, already. Not everything had to be so serious.

He wasn't taking this situation seriously enough.

Randy stacked the final box in the storeroom and locked up. He'd talked to Austin earlier, like he had each day his brother had been gone, but Austin hadn't been forthcoming with information. Mostly, his brother wanted specifics about the cattle. It was kind of annoying. Randy needed answers. Like what was wrong and when would he be back?

And now Hannah was coming over to see the house.

So much for being careful around her.

He'd give her the tour, they'd have a slice of pizza, and that would be that.

He strode to his truck. Inside, he sat for a minute before starting it up. Did a brief self-check. His breathing was normal. His pulse was, too. Heart rate didn't feel out of whack. Earlier, he'd been so stressed about corralling the calf, he'd feared his heart was going to explode.

And Hannah was a little too perceptive for his taste. Another reason he needed Austin back—Randy wouldn't have to worry about her all-too-seeing eyes.

On stressful days like this, he usually wound down by driving out to one of his favorite fishing spots, but he hadn't been fishing in weeks. And he wouldn't be tonight, either.

Driving down Main Street, Randy thought of Ned. That dog of hers sure had found a way into his heart in all of two seconds flat. There was something soothing and comforting about dogs. They didn't judge. Just looked at you and accepted you. Licked your hand. Wagged their tails.

Yeah, dogs were the best, and Ned was extra special.

Swinging by Dino's Pizza, Randy bought one of their grab-and-go pepperoni pizzas and headed to the house. Anticipation built when he turned into the drive. Rounding the bend, he spotted Hannah's Jeep.

When she'd mentioned bringing Ned here, he'd instantly wanted to show off the new house to her. He was proud of it—proud of what it represented. His own life. On his terms.

He got out of the truck, grabbed the pizza and the mini-cooler he'd stocked earlier. A rush of satisfaction filled him as he took in the home. Dark gray siding climbed the two-story structure. Stone masonry covered much of the first floor. White porch rails, a white door and white shutters set off the gray, giving the home a welcoming touch.

He didn't see Hannah in the Jeep or in the front yard. She must have Ned out back. He let himself inside and set the pizza on one of the unopened cabinet boxes in the kitchen. The cabinets he'd hoped would be installed today.

There was nothing he could do about the delay. He opened the sliding door and stepped out onto the deck.

Hannah tossed a ball beyond Ned, who chased after it and brought the ball back to her, dropping it at her feet. Randy watched them for a while, surprised to see her like this. He was used to her bubbly, sunny personality. Used to her laughter, her teasing, her bringing people into a conversation.

He wasn't used to seeing her completely carefree. Ned seemed to be loving this side of her, too.

Why was a girl like her still single?

He didn't need or want the answer.

"Oh!" She looked up and waved. "I didn't see you there."

"Hungry?" He propped his forearms on the deck rail. She gave the dog a treat from her pocket then strode to the deck's stairs with Ned loping beside her.

"Yes, I'm famished." With a tote bag in hand, she reached the top step, her face flushed and eyes sparkling. Ned zoomed to Randy, sitting and staring up at him. He chuckled, petting the dog. "Want to eat out here?"

"Um, yeah. Duh."

"I'll be right back." He went to the garage, grabbed two of the camping chairs he kept on hand and unfolded them on the deck. Then he brought out the cooler, handed her a soda and set the pizza on top of the cooler.

Hannah took the paper plates out of her tote bag and handed him one along with a napkin. They sat side by side with the cooler and pizza between them, facing his big backyard. Ned stretched out, resting his doggy chin on his paws near Randy's feet.

"This property…" Hannah faced him. "I'm speechless. It's absolutely perfect. I never imagined it was this private."

A rush of pride filled him. It meant a lot to hear her praise. He loved it, too. The mountains stood in a jagged outline against the blue sky. The trees beyond the stream gave the land privacy sorely lacking in this area. It was as if his house were the only one around for miles.

"Just think, you can have your morning coffee out here and watch the wildlife sneaking through your yard. You know they'll be heading to the stream. Are there fish in it?"

He could picture it, too. He'd already seen deer and a fox. "Yeah, it's great for trout. All kinds of species. I'll be testing my lures on them."

"Will you do your videos out there, too?"

He was surprised. "You watch my videos?"

"I've seen one or two."

Huh. Imagine that. Hannah had watched his videos. What did she think when she saw him online?

"I hadn't thought of filming out here, but I probably could." What would it take? A tripod and camera. He had those. "It would give me a chance to show how various techniques work."

"And it would let people see the beauty of Wyoming."

That it would. They ate in relaxed silence for a while.

"I didn't realize the store was so busy," she said. "How did you come to own it?"

Not many people asked him about it. "I fell in love with fishing when I was a little kid. Begged Dad to sign me up for competitions. Competed all through high school." His heart twinged with mixed emotions. "But then Dad died, and I had to help with the ranch."

"I'm sorry."

"It's okay. It was a long time ago."

"Still. Losing your parents—you don't really get over it, do you?"

He supposed not.

"So you and Austin took over the ranch," she said. "Then what?"

"Then I missed fishing. Missed the competitions. Started buying all the latest lures and going off to local spots on my downtime. One day Austin walked into the spare room where I'd been stacking boxes of fishing supplies, and he got all huffy, saying I could open a store with all that stuff."

Hannah shifted in her seat to face him, and her face glowed with interest. It had been a while since anyone hung on his words. More than a while, actually. A guy could get used to it.

"And the rest is history?" she asked.

"Not quite. But the idea was there. And it grew. For the first time in my life, I got serious about my future. Researched how to run a business, listed what I'd need. Kept my eye out for one of the buildings to go up for rent. Talked to the bank. And when I'd done all the legwork, my worst task still loomed."

She gave him a questioning stare.

"My brother. I had to break it to Austin I wasn't going to ranch anymore. He didn't take it well."

"No, I suppose he wouldn't."

"We worked it out. Figured out an equitable way to deal with the ranch and the money involved. I opened the store. And then the rest was history."

She stared into the distance, her profile serious. He wanted to ask what she was thinking, but what guy did that? One looking for trouble.

"It took a lot of guts," she said, turning to him again. "Telling Austin you weren't ranching. Starting the store."

She thought he had guts? His chest was probably puffing out to ridiculous proportions.

Sitting out here, eating pizza, sharing personal stuff wasn't a good move, though. Maybe Austin being gone had turned him into a softy or something. Whatever was happening to him, he'd better put an end to it.

He stood abruptly. "You ready for the tour?"

"Yep." They gathered the used plates and pizza box and went back inside with Ned.

Randy led her to the front entryway where an open staircase stood to the right and a large living room was to the left. The flooring hadn't been installed yet, but the walls had been primed with white paint.

"This is where I'll spend most of my time." He took her through the living room and back to the kitchen, answering questions along the way. Large boxes lined the wall. "They're supposed to be installing the cabinets this week."

"What color?"

"White."

"What's this?" She pointed to a door.

"Garage." He brushed past her to open it, once again noticing her perfume. A spick-and-span three-car garage greeted them. "Probably the cleanest it will ever be."

She chuckled, pointing to another door. "And this?"

"Half bath here. Basement there. It's a walkout. I won't be finishing it anytime soon, though." He escorted her down the hall again and up the stairs. "I've got my hands full with everything else."

A landing large enough for a small sitting area stood at the top. Then he showed her two good-sized bedrooms, a full bath and a laundry room. Finally, they went into the master bedroom with its big walk-in closet, large windows and another full bathroom. The space was huge. The way he liked it. Would give him space to think. To spread out.

By himself.

He frowned. Did one person need this much space?

"I love this house." Hannah beamed. "Love the exterior, the layout. And this master bath? It's amazing." She turned her full attention to him. "Are you seriously going to start painting tonight?"

"Yeah. I've got to get it done."

She nodded. "Well, what room are we painting first?"

*We?* He should have known she'd offer to help. "Uh, I know you had a long day. I didn't mean for you to actually paint when we were joking around earlier."

"I don't mind. I changed into my old clothes before coming here."

"Yes, but—"

"It's a big job to do alone." She gave him the you're-being-dumb look she'd given him countless times over the years. It brought some of his equilibrium back. "Just tell me where you're starting."

*No, no, no...* "The living room."

Were his mouth and brain connected anymore? Why did he keep saying the opposite of what he should? They headed back downstairs, their footsteps loud on the bare steps.

"What color are you painting it?" she asked.

"Beige."

"Please tell me the name of the paint color is not beige." She looked offended.

"No. It's Burst of Champagne or something equally ridiculous."

"Phew." She pretended to wipe her brow.

He continued to the garage and brought in the correct can of paint, rollers, tape and other supplies he'd bought.

"Let me see this." She pointed to the can.

He turned it upside down a few times and pried the lid off.

"Ooh, pretty." She grinned. "If you have a regular brush, I can cut in the paint along the ceiling. Then you can follow me with the roller."

Hannah was helping him paint, and for some dumb reason, he was glad he hadn't gotten rid of her. Just as he knew he was opening up a can of something a whole lot more dangerous than paint by having her stick around.

Whatever she'd been expecting from Randy's house, that wasn't it. It was the sort of house she'd select if she were going to build a home.

After leaving his place, Hannah headed to her parents' ranch. It was still light out, and she had a hankering to talk to her mother. Why she'd had it in her head Randy was building a small house suitable for a bachelor, she didn't know. She'd figured he'd go the rustic route. A log cabin with deer heads on the walls, not the charming picture of domesticity he'd shown her.

For some reason, the contentment she'd enjoyed for the past couple of hours at Randy's had changed into something unfamiliar. Something kind of hard. And painful.

Was she…jealous?

Of Randy?

No. It had been a long day. She probably just needed a good night's sleep. Of all the negative traits she possessed, envy wasn't one. At least, she hadn't thought she was an envious person. Until now.

Mom would help straighten her head out. Hannah had texted her before leaving Randy's.

She parked near the house and let Ned out of the back seat. With two knocks on the side door, she let herself inside and headed straight to the kitchen.

"How's it going at the store, honey?" Mom opened an upper cabinet. "Want some iced tea? Or hot? It's cool out there tonight."

"Hot tea sounds good." Hannah pulled out a stool and sat at the counter. Dad came into the room and grinned.

"Hey, there. I see you brought my favorite dog." He crouched to pet Ned. "What a good boy. I got you some treats." Dad used his goofy Grandpa tone with Ned. The tough old cowboy was a pushover when it came to dogs and kids.

"What about me?" Hannah pretended to be hurt.

"You want a dog treat, too?" His eyes twinkled.

"You love my dog more than me, don't you?" She wagged her finger. "I remember a time not long ago when you would have had a candy bar for me. Now it's fun stuff for Ned."

"What can I say? I like your dog. And I did pick up a few toys for him. Ned and I are going to check them out while you and your mother gab." He gestured to Ned, and the dog eagerly joined him as they left the room.

Mom set a steaming mug in front of her and sat on a stool facing her. "Any word from Austin?"

"Not that I know of." It was practically killing her mother not to know why Austin had left town. Hannah was curious about it, too. "But I did get to tour Randy's house tonight."

"Oh?" The vowel swung up on the end. She probably shouldn't be getting Mom's hopes up by mentioning a single man and his new house in the same sentence.

"It's really nice. Incredible view." Hannah described the layout, and as she did the yucky feeling from the drive worsened.

Randy was going to live in that beautiful home. He had a thriving business. His YouTube videos drew an audience from all over the world. She knew because she'd checked.

"Seems a shame for him to live in a big house all by his lonesome." Mom made a clucking sound as she stirred her tea.

"Well, it doesn't seem to bother him."

"Hmm."

"I mean he's proud of it. I didn't get the impression he would have it any other way." Was there an edge to her voice?

"Does that bother you?"

"No. Of course not."

"Hmm."

"What's with all the *hmm*s?" Hannah was getting annoyed. "You usually have a lot to say."

"Maybe he's ready for the next step. After living with his brother all these years, it's probably for the best they're getting separate homes. Now they can get wives, start families."

Hannah refrained from rolling her eyes. Everything ended in marriage and kids in her mom's mind. But in real life, it didn't work that way.

"It sounds like Randy has his life together," Mom said. "I'm happy for him."

He did. He had it all together. Randy had it all going on.

Her chest squeezed.

It wasn't as if she didn't. She'd be the first to admit she had more blessings than most.

"He deserves the house," Hannah said, trying to muster a better attitude. "He has a successful business, good friends. I'm happy for him." The last part she'd had to drag out of her mouth.

"You don't sound very happy." Mom peered over the rim at her.

"Well, I am. I have a great apartment." She shook her head. "I love my job. And now I have Ned."

"Hmm."

If her mother *hmm*'d one more time…

"Randy's house has nothing to do with me." The thought of those empty rooms and him padding around the home by himself made her sigh. He seemed to be fine with being single. In fact, he seemed to be embracing it.

And the truth was she did have blessings, but she didn't want to be alone for the rest of her life. And the little time she'd spent with him lately had made her all too aware of it.

"So what do you have going on this week?" Hannah changed the subject.

Her mom took the hint, mentioning watching Sunni and Cam for Hannah's brother Michael and her sister-in-law Leann tomorrow afternoon, but Mom's watchful eyes told her she knew something was up.

Hannah wasn't ready to face these new revelations. Not when she'd been doing so well at pretending they didn't exist. Randy intrigued her. She didn't know him as well as she thought she did. And that was a danger sign. One she'd ignored in the past and wouldn't again.

## Chapter Three

$F$riday afternoon Randy opened the back door to the shop, pausing in the hallway as he heard Hannah's voice coming from the front.

"No, I'm not going to Erica's wedding tomorrow. She had to keep her end of the guest list smaller than she wanted since it's out of town. At least it saved me from having to fill out the plus-one box. No date for me... What? Oh, no, I'm not bringing anyone to Tess's wedding. Come on, you know better than that." Her tone was playful, but an edge of pain accompanied it.

Randy frowned. Before last week, he'd generally not thought about Hannah much. Hadn't allowed himself to. But now he'd been thinking about her more and more. Every night after work the two of them had grabbed some takeout and headed to his house to paint. With her help, they'd finished painting all but three rooms.

It had been easy being with her.

He really should find a way to repay her for all she'd done this week.

"I'll be fine," she said. "I've been to seven weddings in the past two years. I'm more than familiar with the singles table. The great aunt, weird cousin, awkward coworker—I've dealt with them all…" Her throaty laugh made him chuckle under his breath. He began walking in her direction. Seven weddings? He shivered. Leave it to Hannah to make the best of an uncomfortable situation. "…if all the groomsmen are bringing dates, I told Tess to sit me with one of my brothers. I'll be fine."

One of her brothers? Not on his watch.

He could tell from the way her voice cracked at the end she wouldn't be fine. And it bothered him.

It shouldn't bother him, though. Wasn't his place to care.

He emerged into the main store. Ned uncurled himself and came up to him, his tongue lolling in what appeared to be a smile. "Hey, there, buddy."

"Oh, hey, gotta go…Yeah, see you soon." Hannah hung up and turned to him, her cheeks rosy. "Didn't hear you come in."

"Just got here." She'd sacrificed every waking minute this week to help him out and asked for nothing in return. Yeah, he was paying her by the hour, but she wasn't helping him for the money. He should do something nice for her. But what?

Her eyelids lowered as she pointed to the counter. "Well, I took it upon myself to take care of all the invoices. They're in the binder. And here's the list of items getting low. You'll have to order more soon." She tore off the top page of a notepad and handed it to him.

He didn't bother looking at it. "Do you have plans tonight?"

"No, why?" She narrowed her eyes.

"Want to come out to the ranch? I'll grill some steaks.

Ned will like it out there." He glanced down at the dog, still glued to his side.

With a slight shrug, she smiled. "Okay. When?"

"How about now?" Thanks to her, he had no unfinished business to deal with in the store. It was as if she could run it with her hands tied behind her back. Humbled him, if he were being honest.

"Yeah, okay." She called Ned's name, and he went straight to her. After clipping on his leash, she gathered her purse and tote bag. "I guess I'll see you over there."

After locking up, he followed her out and drove behind her all the way to the ranch. The summer sky made the prairie pop to life. Purple coneflowers, green grass, sagebrush and tall grasses flowed past in a colorful blur. Soon, the plains would be dry and the colors would fade.

As much as he tried to forget it, Hannah's phone conservation kept replaying in his mind.

Why wasn't she dating anyone? Why had she attended seven—how was it even possible to be invited to seven?—weddings by herself? Hannah had always seemed like an open book to him—still did—but maybe she had a box full of disappointments locked inside her the way he did.

He turned down the long gravel lane leading to the farmhouse. Her Jeep pulled to a stop at the side of the house. Right next to Austin's truck.

Randy's pulse started to race.

Austin was back. *Yes!*

No more dealing with wayward calves, crabby cows or piles of manure. Although, he had to admit, working on the ranch all week reminded him of things he'd never thought he'd miss, like riding out with Dad and Austin, spending hours in the saddle with nothing to do but think.

No phone to scroll through. No orders to place. No customers interrupting him.

Still, he was glad Austin was back. But anxiety sped up his heartbeat, too. Whatever Austin's emergency had been, it must have been big.

Hannah and Ned stood near the bottom of the porch, and he loped over to them. "Austin's back."

"We can do this another time." She lightly bit the bottom corner of her lip as the front door opened. Austin stood in the doorway. A weird squeal came from inside the house.

"I've never been so happy to see you in my life." In the shadows, Austin was leaning on something and waved for them to come in. "Hannah, I need your help."

Hannah? Randy blinked. Why would he need Hannah? A flood of sensations overwhelmed him, and Ned began licking Randy's hand. He gripped the porch rail to steady himself as a moment of dizziness came over him. Then he and Ned entered the house and continued down the hall to the kitchen where his feet screeched to a halt.

Hannah was lifting a baby out of a car seat.

A baby?

Randy looked at Austin, who was leaning on crutches and murmuring something to Hannah.

"Why are you on crutches? Why is there a baby here? What's going on?" Randy heard the words come out of his mouth but had no concept he'd spoken them.

"Sit down." Austin nodded to the kitchen table. "I'll explain."

"I think this little one needs a diaper change." Hannah beamed at the baby she held up near her face. The sight of her holding the infant dropped the bottom out of

Randy's stomach. It was an image he knew he'd never be able to erase from his mind.

Hannah and babies went together.

"The diaper bag is right here. I'd do it but…" Austin's face had grown tomato red.

"You can't change the baby on crutches, silly." She let out a tinkly laugh. "I'll be right back with this cutie."

"What. Is. Going. On?" Randy's heart ramped to a jackhammer pace, and a wet feeling on his hand made him aware Ned was licking him again.

"Why don't you sit down?"

Good idea.

He stalked over to the table, yanked out a chair and sat. Ned laid his head in his lap, and Randy stroked his soft fur as he slowly calmed down. Austin awkwardly lowered himself onto the chair opposite, setting the crutches next to him. They stared at each other for a long moment. Hannah, carrying the baby, bounced back into the room.

Her eyes grew round as she backed up a step. "I'll leave you two alone."

"Could you stay?" Austin asked. "Just for a while. I…I need help."

Randy had never heard him sound this desperate. Asking for help? Not barking out orders?

"Of course," she said quietly, taking a seat and cradling the baby in her arms.

"This is my son. Austin Junior—AJ." His face turned a pale shade of green. "His mother died last week."

"Wait—what?" Randy sorted through his memories. "You don't even have a girlfriend. You haven't left the ranch in months. How did you manage to fit in getting a girl pregnant?"

"I go to Texas twice a year." Austin's flat tone brought

Randy back to reality. He'd forgotten about that. Austin had never told him why he was going. Just left on a Friday afternoon and came back on a Sunday night. Randy hadn't realized it was for a girl.

He stared at Austin. Did he know his brother at all?

"Why didn't you tell me you had a girlfriend? That she was pregnant? That you have a son?"

"I didn't know!" All the fight seemed to fizzle from Austin.

"What's her name? How long were you together?" Randy tried to piece the puzzle together and failed miserably.

"Her name was Camila Rodriguez. She was in the navy. An adventure junkie. Her job was disarming explosive devices."

Hannah let out a whistling sound. Randy was tempted to do the same. Camila sounded way too exciting for by-the-book Austin. Maybe the saying *opposites attract* had some truth to it.

"Is that how she died?" she asked.

Austin shook his head, clenching his jaw. "No, she had a stroke. Routine deep diving exercises at sea. They couldn't revive her."

All three of them were silent for a few moments.

"Did you know about the baby?" Randy asked. He had to know. Had to make sense of the man and his secrets sitting across from him with the upright brother he'd lived his entire life with.

"I knew." His face looked haggard.

"And you didn't plan to be in his life?" He hated his judgmental tone, but he couldn't stop it from coming out of his mouth.

"I'm not going into it right now, okay? All that mat-ters is this is my son, I have sole custody, I sprained my ankle and I need help."

Help? Randy knew what that meant, and his spirits plunged to the depths of the earth. "I've already been away from the store all week." He shook his head, glancing at Hannah, who was watching them through wide eyes as the baby sucked on a pacifier. "And Hannah's hands are tied with the new dog and the puppy arriving on Sunday. She's already given up a lot of her time."

Austin let out a frustrated sigh. "I know, but I can't exactly do ranch chores on crutches. You're going to have to keep managing it for me. I'll be off them in a week. Two, at the most. It's a light sprain, but if I mess it up now, I'll be off my feet a lot longer than two weeks."

Anger and irritation bubbled up Randy's throat. "So what are you suggesting? Bo's still in Alabama. Finn's not coming back for another week. You want me to run the ranch. Who's going to run the store? Who's going to take care of the baby?"

The way his chest tightened warned him his blood pressure was soaring. Ned licked his arm. At least someone here seemed to sympathize with him.

"I'll take care of the baby." Hannah's voice—barely a whisper—filled the room.

Randy stifled a groan. He wasn't surprised. But he couldn't let her do this.

He was supposed to be repaying her for her help, not roping her into even more work.

"No way." Randy shook his head. "You are *not* taking care of the baby."

"Why not?" Austin bellowed.

Hannah's heart ached for these men she'd known her

entire life. They were stuck in a strange, tough situation, and if her experience with two stubborn older brothers had taught her anything, life wouldn't get normal for them for a good, long while. At least she could make sure the baby was getting the care he needed and deserved while they hashed it out.

She stared at AJ and her heart grew lighter. His lips formed an oval as he yawned, the pacifier almost falling out of his mouth. What a sweetheart. How she loved babies.

But what about the puppy? She was picking up the little guy in two days. Could she really handle Ned, a baby and a puppy?

Well, she did teach elementary school. If she could handle a classroom full of third graders, she could probably take on all this, too.

"Haven't you heard a word I said?" Randy glared at his brother. "We're already in her debt."

Her debt? Hardly.

"It's what friends do, Randy," she said. "They help each other out. And it will only be until you guys can hire a nanny." She started sorting through possible people in the area to hire to babysit AJ. None came to mind off the top of her head. "Austin, can you drive?"

"Yes. The sprain's in my left ankle." He actually looked sheepish.

So Austin could drive but couldn't do ranch chores or take care of the baby. And Randy needed someone to take care of the store. She would watch the baby, but what about the rest?

The solution was so close. It was just out of her grasp. Then everything fell into place.

She tightened her hold on the darling boy and looked at Austin. "You'll run Randy's store."

Then she turned to Randy. "And you're going to have to keep dealing with the ranch for the time being." She addressed Austin again. "Two weeks?"

He grunted. "One, if I have anything to say about it."

She arched her eyebrows and nodded. "So at least a week. And I'll take care of the baby."

"It's not fair to you, Hannah," Randy said. "You've got the puppy coming, and…"

"I'll bring it with me. It's good to get them used to new environments." She beamed down at the baby. Surely, she could handle taking care of AJ and the puppy for a week. "And I know all the teenage girls in this area. Trust me, they'll want to help out with babysitting. You two are going to need some help until you get used to having a baby around and can hire a nanny."

Austin visibly relaxed. His head tipped back, and he let out a loud sigh. "Thank you, Hannah."

AJ began to fuss. She assumed he was hungry.

"Why don't I get a bottle ready?" She rose, walking over to Austin and setting the babe in his arms. His face softened as he stared at the child. It told her everything she needed to know. Whatever his reasons for not being involved in the baby's life before this, he would be a great daddy.

Randy got up quickly and joined her as she went to the living room to get the diaper bag.

"It's too much." He blocked her path to the kitchen. "You already gave up all your free time and then some last week."

"I wanted to." She dug through the diaper bag for a bottle. "And I want to help you now. The poor baby lost his mother. His daddy is out of commission. AJ needs extra love. I'm happy to give it to him. And trust me, Mom will be coming over, too. You can't keep her away when there's an emergency or a baby."

He seemed to chew on the thought. "What am I going to do, Hannah?"

"About what?" She found a bottle and a canister of formula.

"Austin can barely get around. And this baby—how old do you think he is?"

"I don't know. Let's ask." She craned her neck around him. "Hey, Austin," she called, "how old is AJ?"

"Thirteen weeks," he yelled from the other room.

"Do babies this young sleep through the night?" Randy's forehead resembled the Grand Canyon the grooves were so deep. She wanted to run her finger over them. Soothe his worries.

"Some do." She pushed past him into the kitchen with him practically tripping over her as he followed.

"I've never changed a diaper. What if he cries? How much do they eat?"

She stopped in front of the sink and looked back at him. He looked positively ill. Ned zoomed over. The dog always seemed to come around when Randy was worked up. Maybe the dog was picking up on his anxiety cues the same way he'd sensed his previous owner's health issues.

"Relax." She spun to face him, placing her palms against his chest. His heartbeat was pounding, and his muscles twitched. She pulled her hands away, trying to ignore the way his strong muscles felt. "You're going to be fine. I'll show you how to change him and feed him."

She turned back to the task at hand—getting a bottle

ready—but touching Randy had set off those flutters in her stomach again.

They returned to the table, and she handed Austin the bottle. He thanked her and gave it to AJ, who let out a contented sigh and began to drink.

"Do you have anything for the baby besides the diaper bag?" She held her breath. What if Austin had no real supplies for AJ?

"The truck is full. I packed all his stuff and brought it with me. Had to take the crib and changing table apart to get them here, though. Thankfully, I got everything done before I twisted my ankle."

"I'll get started unloading it." Randy left the room.

Hannah turned to go help him. First, though, she set her hand on Austin's shoulder. "You're going to be a great daddy. AJ's a beautiful little boy."

His muscles tensed, and he covered her hand with his own for a brief moment. Then she left the room.

Something told her these brothers were going to need a lot of support for the next couple of weeks. And she was glad to give it to them.

She'd just have to keep reminding herself this wasn't her family. Wasn't her baby. They'd get through it fine, and afterward, she'd be on her own again. Just her and the dogs.

How could his brother keep this from him?

A secret girlfriend. A secret baby.

Randy unlocked the truck's bed cover and folded it back, revealing the boxes and furniture inside. *Keep busy. Unload. Don't think about it.* All the emotions churning up threatened to spill over.

Regardless of how many arguments they'd gotten into

over the years, Randy had always, always told Austin the truth.

Except about... That was different.

His secret was private. Personal.

He dragged out the first box and carried it to the porch. Where were they going to set up the baby's room? The spare room, probably.

He couldn't think about it, yet. He placed the box on the porch, went back to the truck, pulled some plastic contraption out and hauled it to the porch, too.

Hannah came outside with Ned, the screen door slamming behind her.

He was still blown away by her generosity. What woman offered all her free time like that?

A giving one. A kind one.

The image earlier of her holding AJ as if he were the most precious thing in the world came back.

The sort of woman who was meant to get married and have a bunch of her own babies.

His spirits dropped. In another life, he might have been first in line to be that guy. But it wouldn't be fair to her or any kids he might have.

The heart condition that had killed his father would kill him, too.

He had no idea when. All he knew was he'd inherited hypertrophic cardiomyopathy from his dad.

Randy would never forget the day he'd walked into Dad's bedroom and found him dead. Forty-eight years old. Young. Healthy. In shape.

Then gone.

Randy had lived with the trauma for years. And he would never put someone he loved through that. Never.

"What can I help with?" Hannah joined him at the tailgate.

"Can you ask Austin where he wants the baby's stuff set up?" He couldn't look at her. Couldn't take the chance she'd somehow sense his heart was a ticking time bomb waiting to explode, taking him down for good.

"Sure. Be right back."

Ned sat next to him, watching him. He looked down at the dog. "Why do I get the feeling you can read my thoughts and your owner can, too?"

The dog thumped his tail.

"You didn't answer my question, Ned." Randy grabbed another box and hefted it over to the porch, then pivoted to get a fresh load.

"He said the spare room." Hannah bounded back down the steps. "Why don't you take a break? Sit for a minute."

"I've been sitting." His veins were straining with the need to do something. Anything.

She took his hand, tugged on it gently and led him to the top step. They sat next to each other, neither speaking.

"It's a lot to take in," she said after a while. She still held his hand, squeezing it softly.

The gesture tore at him, made all the emotions he'd been stuffing deep inside yearn to come out.

"Are you going to be okay with this arrangement?" she asked. "I know you hate ranching."

"I don't hate it. But it's not my passion. It was Austin's and Dad's." That, at least, was a safe topic. He didn't dare discuss the fact his world had just flipped upside down.

"I get it."

He knew she'd understand. And he appreciated her changing the topic to something safer. "That and the fact I'm not as patient as Austin. I get frustrated when the cattle rebel."

"The cattle rebel?" She chuckled. "Dad never mentioned rebellions when I rode out with him."

His mood lightened a notch. Hannah had grown up on a ranch east of town. She was no stranger to cattle.

"Those stinkers get something in their head," he said. "And it's all you can do to move them in the right direction. And try to help one of the mama's precious calves? You're done for."

"You're a good man, Randy." She nudged her elbow into his side.

A good man. Not really. But he wanted to be.

A good man would send Hannah on her way right now. She'd made his life as easy as a summer breeze this week. And she was volunteering to make a mountain of problems disappear in the next couple of weeks.

His heart condition would kill him. He didn't know when. Could be tomorrow. Could be in forty years. But he'd never put a wife through the horror of finding him dead, and he wouldn't take the chance of passing it on to a child, either.

He wasn't the marrying kind. And Hannah was.

But what did he know? He thought his brother was the most upright, honest man he'd ever met. And he'd been wrong about him.

Maybe he didn't know anyone, including Hannah.

And to be fair, she didn't really know him, either.

"You're really okay with taking care of AJ?" he asked.

"I am." Her eyes crinkled in the corners as she smiled up at the sky. "Beats talking to Joe Schlock for hours every day."

He couldn't help it. He laughed. "Austin will be stuck with him."

She touched his hand again. "It's all going to be okay, you know. In a few weeks, everything will be back to normal."

For her, maybe. Randy clenched his jaw. But not for him. A baby changed things.

"Why don't we take a break from this and you can hold your nephew? You can get to know him." She brushed off her legs as she stood, holding out her hand. He took it and rose. "You're going to fall in love with that baby. Just wait and see."

He hoped she was right. He was an uncle now. Whether he was ready or not.

# Chapter Four

"I still can't get over Austin having a baby." Hannah's mom oozed excitement in the passenger seat of the Jeep the next morning. Last night before Hannah left, Austin had asked if she thought her mother might be willing to stop by today to give him some tips on taking care of AJ. Hannah, of course, had assured him Mom would love to help out. She'd been correct.

And while Mom could certainly handle showing him the ropes of child care on her own, Hannah had insisted on coming along. She was worried about Randy. He'd been so shocked, so out of sorts last night. Had he adjusted at all to the fact Austin had a son?

"It's hard to believe he had a girlfriend none of us knew about." Mom kept a loose hold on the container of cupcakes sitting on her lap. A casserole and rolls were nestled on the back seat.

"I know." Hannah glanced at her. "I can't remember the last girl he dated. I guess now we know why."

Something seemed strange about the scenario, though. Austin wasn't the "love 'em and leave 'em" type any more than Randy, Mac or the Mayer brothers were. For him to turn his back on a baby? Well…it didn't add up to the Austin they all knew. He had a loyal streak a mile wide.

"It was nice of the boys to ask me to come out and help." Her mother was clearly tickled he had requested her help over that of any of the other ladies he could have asked.

"I'm not surprised." She gave her mom a quick smile. "You've always treated them like family."

"Yes. In some ways they are. When their father died so unexpectedly, it shook me. I couldn't bear the thought of those two without a mom or dad. Randy was so young, barely out of high school. It made me think about you kids. And well, I hoped the local ladies would look out for you if something like that happened to Dad and me. So in a way, I've considered them part of our family for a long, long time."

All the times Hannah had complained about dropping off baked goods to Austin and Randy soured in her stomach. She'd never really put two and two together concerning her mom and the Watkins brothers. Now that her mother had spelled it out for her, she had a whole new respect for the woman.

"I hope I grow up to be just like you, Mom." She meant it, too.

"Not *just* like me. You can skip my faults."

"Nope. I love you just the way you are."

"If you weren't driving, I'd hug you 'til you squirmed free."

Hannah laughed and turned into the long drive of the ranch. A sea of green grass spread out on either side. Cattle roamed in the distance, and she could make out two riders on horseback near the herd. Probably Randy and another cowboy.

She swallowed her disappointment. So much for finding out how he was handling his new status as an uncle.

After parking near the house, she helped her mom carry the food up the porch steps, then knocked on the door. The sound of a baby crying reached them before the door opened.

"You made it." Randy let out a dramatic sigh and stepped aside for them to enter. Her heart jumped at seeing him. It must have been ranch hands out there on horseback. His hair was disheveled and his eyes were puffy. The T-shirt he wore had spit-up dribbling down the shoulder where he held AJ, who was wailing. "Come in."

"Here, let me." Mom set the cupcakes on top of Hannah's stack of food and held out her arms. Relief washed over his face as she took AJ. She cradled the child, murmuring to him as she headed to the living room. His cries dimmed to a whimper.

"Who's taking care of the cattle?" Hannah toed off her shoes in the hallway. He looked exhausted.

"Toby and Luke." He raked his fingers through his hair. "I don't know what we'd do without them. I mean, I planned on helping this morning, but AJ was up all night, and Austin kept clip-clopping on those crutches to the crib. I actually caught him attempting to pick up the baby—he could have broken his leg! Anyway, I feel like three-day-old roadkill in the middle of a heat wave, and I probably look and smell like it, too."

Hannah bit her lip to keep from laughing. Randy wasn't trying to be funny, but the wild look in his eyes and the way the story tumbled out amused her.

She leaned toward him and sniffed. "Don't worry, you smell okay. Where's Austin?"

He gestured to the staircase. "He's getting dressed. He'll be down in a minute."

"He's staying upstairs?" She led the way to the kitchen and set the food on the counter. "With crutches?"

"Yeah, he is. Dumb, I know. I told him to take the couch, but would he listen? No. Has to be near the baby."

She reached out to touch his forearm. "Are you doing okay? You know, with having a baby around and all this new—"

"I'm fine." His clipped words forced her to drop the subject. For now. The *clunk-clunk* of Austin's crutches made them both retreat to the living room.

"Thanks, Miss Patty." Austin hobbled on one crutch down the remaining stairs as he held on to the rail with the other. "I'm sorry to ask you to come out here, but I figure if anyone knows a thing or two about babies, it's you."

Mom shifted AJ in her arms and met Austin in the middle of the room. She reached up and kissed his cheek. "Those grandkids keep me busy. You've got a beautiful boy here, Austin. He's handsome like his daddy."

"Thank you." His face flushed as he nodded.

"Go on and sit down," Mom said. "Let's figure out what you need help with."

Austin sat on one end of the couch, and Mom, holding AJ, sat on the other. Randy plunked down on the recliner, kicked up the footrest, leaned back and groaned, closing his eyes. Hannah perched on the love seat.

"I've got the feeding part down." Austin rubbed his chin. "I think."

Randy lifted his head slightly. "Me, too."

"And I can change a diaper."

"Not me," Randy chimed in. "I tried twice. Didn't work."

Austin blew out a breath. "I don't know how to give him a bath. I don't really know what to do with a kid this young. Where do I sit him? Or do I hold him all the time? He's so small. I'm afraid he'll break. Am I supposed to be teaching him stuff? He cries a lot, and I wish he could tell me what's wrong."

Her mom kept a straight face as she nodded. Hannah held her laughter in, but it was hard.

"I can help with all that," Mom said. "We'll give him a bath together so you know how to do it. And he looks about three months old—"

"He is," Austin said. "Thirteen weeks."

"Good, he'll like a bouncy chair. He'll need some time on his tummy, too, to get his little back and limbs strong. Where is he sleeping?"

"In the spare room."

"In a crib or…" From the looks of it, Mom had a thousand questions on the tip of her tongue.

"Why don't I show you?" Randy snapped the footrest down and heaved himself out of the recliner. "I don't have a clue how to set up the room. Could use some pointers."

Mom carried AJ upstairs, and Hannah followed. To the left was a spare bedroom. The crib was in the center of the room. The changing table hadn't been put together yet. A twin bed, dresser and boxes of who-knew-what cluttered the space.

"I need to organize it." Randy frowned, rubbing his chin.

"Is the baby sleeping in the crib?" Mom asked.

"He's not sleeping at all. Every time I set him in there, his eyes pop open and he starts crying again."

"New house. No idea where his mommy went. I'm

not surprised." Mom turned to her. "Here, honey, take the baby."

Hannah's heart skipped a beat at the delight of having AJ back in her arms. He blinked up at her through long, dark lashes. She smiled down at him. "You are precious, aren't you? I can't wait to take care of you all next week."

His brown eyes widened.

"We're going to read stories and cuddle and all kinds of stuff." She cooed, gently tracing his hairline with her fingertip.

Mom was telling Randy where to set up the changing table and how to organize the toys. "And you might want to move the crib over here. Do you have a mobile?"

"A mobile?" His eyebrows dipped together. "What's that?"

"It dangles above the crib. Usually, animals hang and spin as music plays. Although, now that I think of it, Kelli's kids had an electronic screen with the cutest sea creatures you've ever seen scrolling across it. Owen— bless his heart, once he got over the colic—loved watching it before he fell asleep."

"A mobile, huh? I don't know." Randy shrugged. "There might be one in these boxes."

"Don't worry about it now, hon. But it might help him get to sleep. Couldn't hurt to try. And I can ask Kelli if she still has that screen. Did you say you have a baby bathtub?"

"Uh, yeah. I think so." He maneuvered around the boxes to the corner and dug around until he held a small blue tub.

"What about shampoo and lotion? Baby towels?"

Randy started looking overwhelmed again as he massaged the back of his neck. "I don't know. I'll ask Austin." He turned toward the door, but Hannah blocked the doorway.

"Let me," she said. He nodded. She carried AJ down the staircase. Austin sat on the couch with his forehead in his hands. "Hey, you okay?"

He looked up, his eyes clouded with fear and anxiety. "Yeah."

She sat next to him, being careful with the baby, and patted his arm. "It's going to be all right."

"I know." He didn't look or sound convinced.

She needed to lighten the mood.

"Be honest," she teased, "What's bothering you the most—bringing home a baby or spraining your ankle and not being able to check on the cattle?"

He made a half-hearted attempt to smile. "All of it. I haven't been out riding the ranch in over a week. I need to get out there."

Hannah wasn't surprised. She'd grown up with a father who lived, ate and breathed their ranch. Of course Austin was having a hard time with it.

"You'll be out there in no time. Don't worry. Randy and the other cowboys have it under control."

"Yeah." He still didn't look convinced.

Mom and Randy chatted as they came down and put the tub in the dining room before returning to their seats.

"Want me to start putting the word around to hire a nanny?" Hannah asked.

Her mother shook her head. "Before you can even think about hiring a nanny, you need to do some damage control."

Damage control? Hannah was puzzled. Like in the house or...

"Word's going to blaze through Sunrise Bend that

you have a baby." Her mom gave Austin a firm, compassionate look. "I'd advise you to tell those closest to you in person straight away or there will be hurt feelings. And I don't know what you want everyone else in town to know, but decide on what you're telling them now so you're not caught like a possum at night when they all start asking questions."

Austin dropped his head into his hands again. Hannah glanced Randy's way. He stared at his feet.

"I'll tell the guys," Austin said more to himself than anyone.

"Why don't I call them to come over tonight?" Randy pressed his fist to his forehead. "Oh, wait. I keep forgetting. Jet and Blaine left town yesterday for Erica's wedding, and, since Tess is a bridesmaid, Sawyer's gone, too."

"Did Mac go?" Austin asked.

"No, he didn't," Mom said. "Erica had to keep her guest list manageable. I'm surprised she was okay with having the wedding two hours away. That soon-to-be-husband of hers could have been more accommodating."

Hannah and her mother had enjoyed many conversations about the elusive Jamie and if he was the right guy for Erica Mayer.

"Well, should I text Mac to see if he can come over later or not?" Randy pulled out his phone.

"Yeah."

"Austin, let me know when you want to start looking for a nanny." Hannah shifted the baby to make him more comfortable, and he snuggled back into her arms. Best feeling in the world.

Austin sat up straight, looking grim. "I'll call Sawyer in a while. He can tell Jet and Blaine for me. And if Mac can come over, I'll tell him tonight. Tomorrow, I'll take AJ to church. Everyone will see I have a baby. I'll answer the questions once and be done with it. Randy, can you come to church with me?"

He was typing in his phone. "Yep. I'll get up early to do the ranch chores."

"If Randy's doing chores, then Austin, you're going to need some help," Mom said. "I know you can't take care of the baby on your own with that ankle. I'll stop by in the morning. I can feed and change AJ for you. I'll pack up a diaper bag to take to church, too."

Austin had paled. "I'm very thankful, Miss Patty."

"Okay, let's give this little pumpkin a bath." Mom stood, clapped her hands and beamed. "Hannah, you start undressing him while Randy and I get the bath filled up."

Randy followed her mother, and Hannah unsnapped AJ's pajamas, then carefully eased his arms out.

None of this could be easy on Austin or Randy. Her mom was right. Once everyone in town found out about the baby, their lives were bound to get even more complicated.

Randy was a grown man, but last week had been hard on him. And now he had a baby to help take care of on top of the ranch, his store and the projects he needed to finish at the new house.

The pressure was building.

She'd do her best to help alleviate it. Finding a nanny would benefit them all.

Randy's temples throbbed as he let Mac in through the side door that night. It had been a long, demanding, tiring, overwhelming day. He wasn't a bath person, but after seeing how much AJ had loved the warm water,

Randy was tempted to pour himself one to soothe his aching muscles, sore from a week's worth of manual labor.

He couldn't, though. He was on baby duty.

He just prayed the little guy stayed asleep for a while. Twenty minutes ago, AJ had conked out in a bouncy seat Miss Patty had unearthed from one of the boxes. He sent up a silent prayer of thanks for whomever invented that gem of a product.

"Hey, man, good to see you." Mac pulled him into a half embrace and grinned as he entered. "Haven't seen you in a while. How's the house coming along?"

"Slow." They continued to the kitchen, where Austin sat at the table. "I'm supposed to pick out appliances, and I still have three rooms to paint."

Mac grimaced. "I'm all thumbs when it comes to painting, but I'll help if you need me to."

"Hannah helped me cut in the ceilings of most of the rooms. I rolled the walls. I planned on getting the rest done this weekend, but…"

"Oh, Hannah helped you paint, did she?" Mac's grin had a knowing element Randy wanted to wipe right off his face. "She's running the store. She's helping you paint. Next you'll tell me you two are dating."

"We're not dating." Randy ground his teeth together as his face grew hot. "She's doing me a favor."

"Right. A favor. Are you buying this, Austin?" Mac frowned as he took in Austin's appearance. Two days of stubble, hair sticking up, deep circles under his eyes. "Whoa. What happened to you?"

Austin raised bleak eyes. "Sprained my ankle."

"That was your big emergency?" Mac pulled a chair out across from him and sat on it.

"No, just the icing on the cake. I brought home a baby."

"You what?" Mac almost tipped the chair over. He steadied himself.

Austin turned his head to where the baby slept in the bouncy seat on the floor next to him.

Mac rose slightly, peered over the table, then got up and tiptoed to the baby. "There's a real baby in there."

Randy almost rolled his eyes, but he was too tired to make the effort. The past twenty-four hours had been the most demanding of his life. Earlier when Hannah and her mom were there, he'd wanted to drag Hannah outside to rant about everything—the baby, the lack of sleep, the having no clue how to get a diaper to stay on. But he'd done what he always did—shut the feelings down and pretended everything was fine.

Everything was not fine, though.

It wasn't Hannah's problem. It was his, and he'd take care of it himself.

"This is Austin Junior. AJ. He's my boy." A smile brightened Austin's face momentarily. In fact, a touch of pride lined his tone.

Mac stared openmouthed for a long moment at Austin. "You're putting me on."

He shook his head, maintaining eye contact.

"How? Who? When?"

Randy's spirits rose at Mac's incredulous response, and he took a seat at the table as Austin filled him in with the same information he'd given Randy last night.

Randy hadn't worked up the nerve to ask Austin about the mother—Camila—and their relationship. How long had they dated? When did they break up? How could Austin leave her if he'd known she was pregnant? Why wouldn't he have taken responsibility for the child before this?

He had so many questions.

But Hannah and her mom had been there for hours, showing them baby basics and helping him set up the nursery, and there hadn't been time. At least everything was unpacked and in its place. They'd even set up a baby station in the living room with diapers, wipes, toys, burp cloths and all the other things he'd never known about until now.

He wished he still didn't know about them.

It wasn't that he didn't like the baby. He'd have to be a monster not to think the kid was cute. But he didn't have the time or energy to deal with a baby right now. He felt like he'd been thrown into an alternate universe with no instructions on how it worked.

"Do the other guys know about this?" Mac asked Austin. Randy refocused on their conversation.

"I called Sawyer earlier. He's telling Jet and Blaine for me. I didn't want to interrupt the wedding, seeing how they're both in the bridal party."

"So this means you're a single dad." Mac looked stunned, and the weight of it seemed to settle on Austin's shoulders.

"Yeah."

"How's that going to work with the ankle?" Mac pointed to the crutches.

"I won't need them in another week. In the meantime, I'll be manning the store for Randy. He's taking care of the ranch. And Hannah offered to watch the baby until we hire a nanny."

"Which will be soon." Randy gave his brother a stern look.

"I know," Austin snapped. "Why do you keep acting like I'm happy with this? I feel bad enough without needing all your help. If I could throw away the crutches right now, I would."

"That's not what I meant."

"Yeah. I know." Austin's cheek muscle flickered. "I'm just tired is all."

"Join the club," Randy muttered, thinking of the four minutes of sleep he'd gotten all night.

Mac looked at Austin. Then at Randy. And a grin spread across his face. He started to chuckle, and before long, it grew into full-on laughter.

"Quiet down," Randy said, making a downward motion with his hands. "You'll wake him up."

"What?" Austin glared at Mac. "What's so funny?"

"You two. A baby. I can't imagine what the poor kid's going through. I'm amazed he's survived this long. Have either of you even held a baby before?"

"Oh, like you have?" Randy said. Did Mac think it was easy?

"No, but I would have loved to see you trying to take care of him last night."

Austin's lips twitched and a smile burst out. "It was pretty bad."

"Terrible." Randy shook his head, laughter tickling his throat. "Even after Hannah showed me how to put the diaper on, I couldn't do it. The first one I tried was too loose, and AJ destroyed those pajamas. I threw them in the trash next to the stables. I'm sorry, but I'm not going to be a hero with that mess. The next diaper I put on tighter—and I think I cut off his circulation. He has a rash now."

Austin shrugged, looking shell-shocked. "I've been trying to figure out how much the kid eats, and I honestly don't have a clue. I just give him a bottle every time he cries. I don't know what we would do if it wasn't for Miss Patty. She described everything in a way that makes sense."

"Miss Patty came over?" Mac's eyebrows arched.

"Yeah, she gave us a crash course on babies. Explained what he needs, showed us how to set up his room, what to do in the night, how to give him a bath—we'd be lost without her."

"Oh, and she brought cupcakes." Randy pivoted to grab a plastic container off the counter. "Want one?"

"Have I ever turned down her cupcakes?" Mac selected two from the container. Randy grabbed one and set another in front of Austin.

They ate in silence until the baby started making waking-up noises.

At the sound, dread settled into the pit of Randy's stomach. Now he had to figure out what the kid needed again.

He got up and unstrapped the baby, who stretched his tiny arms alongside his ears. His lips formed an O as he blinked awake.

"Hey, there." Randy kept his voice tender, and as soon as he lifted the boy to cradle him, the dread disappeared. Protectiveness gripped him. "Did you have a little nap?"

AJ's baby lips pursed together and began to tremble. Randy prepared for the crying to commence.

"Here." Randy shoved the baby in Mac's arms. "I've got to get a bottle ready."

"Why'd you give him to me?" He looked panicked as he held the baby away from his body awkwardly. AJ started crying in earnest.

"I don't think he needs a bottle," Austin said. "He ate an hour ago."

"Well, genius, what does he need?" Randy paused in the middle of the kitchen with his legs wide. Exasperation burst through his chest. If Austin was so brilliant at this, why was the baby crying?

"What do I do?" Mac held AJ up by his armpits as his face grew red from crying.

"Don't hold him like a bundle of explosives, for one." Austin threw up his hands. "He likes to be held close."

The fear in Mac's eyes was comical. "Like this?" He slowly brought the baby to his shoulder, awkwardly patting his back.

"Yeah, that's a start."

"Why's he still crying?" Mac asked. "This isn't working."

"I'm telling you he needs a bottle." Randy pivoted to get one ready.

"No, he doesn't. Give him the pacifier." Austin rose with the help of his crutch. Then he nosed around the bouncy seat. "Where is it?"

"How am I supposed to know?" Randy didn't mean to snap, but the cries were giving him a headache. His heartbeat pounded as he gripped the edge of the counter, leaned forward and forced himself to take deep breaths.

The crying stopped abruptly. Randy whirled around. Mac still held AJ, who was sucking on a pacifier, and Austin caressed the baby's head.

Crisis averted. The baby was quiet. Calm.

Austin and Mac high-fived each other.

So why was he left with a racing pulse?

And fear.

Raw fear.

This was more than stress, more than adjusting to the baby, more than a disruption to his schedule.

Randy wished Ned were there. The dog helped him feel calm.

Maybe it was time to go back to the doctor. Run those tests he'd put off for years. But what if the doctor told him what he didn't want to hear?

He had to do a better job of managing his stress or he wouldn't be able to help Austin with AJ. He wouldn't be around at all.

They needed him. He couldn't let them down.

## Chapter Five

Puppy day!

Hannah double-checked her tote to make sure she'd packed everything she needed to bring the pup home. She was going to start this puppy-raising adventure off right. Dad had stopped by fifteen minutes ago to pick up Ned. The two dogs could get to know each other later this evening. In the meantime, Ned could enjoy a day with her dad on the ranch.

With her purse over her shoulder, her tote in one hand and the keys in the other, she left the apartment and strolled onto the sidewalk bathed in sunlight.

When she met the puppy, she wanted no distractions. She'd focus on her mission—prepare it to get accepted into the service dog training program.

Maybe the dog would go on to help someone who was blind. Or autistic. Or diabetic. Who knew?

She unlocked her Jeep and climbed in as her cell phone rang. Whoever it was could wait. Randy's name appeared on the screen.

Was something wrong with AJ? She quickly answered it.

"Hey, have you left to get the puppy yet?" He sounded

weird, not himself. Muffled voices mingled in the background.

"No, why? What's wrong?" She set her purse and tote on the passenger seat.

"Want some company?" His voice could only be described as strangled. He lowered it. "The church ladies have been dropping by since the early service ended."

She couldn't stop the grin spreading across her face. "Oh, I see. Dropping off casseroles?"

"That and sticking around to help with the baby. Asking questions. Telling me what I'm doing wrong. Mentioning their single nieces and granddaughters."

She could picture it all, and her smile grew wider. "Is Erma there?"

"Erma and Sally. Dorene just left." He paused. "June, Denise, and Lindy are helping Austin at the moment."

"All three? Yowsers." Hannah started up the Jeep. "You're going to ditch him, aren't you?"

"I have to get out of here." His voice grew desperate. "They'll understand if I say I'm helping you pick up the dog."

"Okay, you big coward." She shook her head, laughing. "Why not tell them you're getting the dog with me, but then slip away to the new house? You can get some work done."

His sigh came through loud and clear. "I would, but…"

"You're not a liar."

"No."

"All right. I'll pick you up. But I'm not going inside, or I'll be late. You know how those ladies like to gab."

"I know. I've experienced hours of it. Hours. I'll wait for you at the end of the drive."

"What? No. Your drive has to be a mile long, if not longer."

"Yeah, so?"

"Whatever you say. See you in a bit." She hung up. He must really be desperate if he was going to wait for her by the ranch's entrance. It was funny to think of him and Austin surrounded by the local matriarchs.

She pulled out of the parking spot and soon was on the road. This wasn't how she'd planned on picking up the puppy. She'd wanted to do it alone. To have this for herself. And, maybe, to do it her way.

Shawn's voice rippled through her head. *You have expectations no one can live up to. You want too much. You're just...too much.*

Was she too much? Were her expectations too high? She turned down the road where the ranch was located. At the time Shawn had said those words, it had been a blow to her heart. And she hadn't pushed back—just accepted he was right. It wasn't as if she hadn't questioned her standards before he came along. Her boyfriend in high school had hinted they were too high.

She had a feeling the guys she'd dated had just been passing time with her until someone better came along.

And she'd been too blind to acknowledge it with Shawn. So busy making her plans, spinning future fantasies of the two of them getting married, buying a house, building a life together, that she'd ignored the obvious.

Shawn couldn't handle her.

So far, no guy could.

Maybe she was too much.

But high expectations weren't such a bad thing. Not when it came to high-stakes situations. Like this puppy.

If she could train it well enough, it could potentially save someone's life.

She spotted Randy up ahead. Slowing, she waited until she reached the ranch entrance before pulling over for him to get in. She moved her tote and purse to the back seat while he got settled.

"Thanks a million, Hannah." He shut the passenger door and buckled his seat belt. "I couldn't take another minute. Sally asked me four times if having AJ around was making me want one of my own. I almost told her having him around was making me never want to have kids. But then she would have told her friends, and it would somehow get turned into me planning on moving a hundred miles away from Austin so I never had to be around AJ again."

"I see your point." She checked her mirrors and merged back on the road. "But AJ couldn't make you not want kids. He's adorable."

"He is cute. He's not the reason I don't want kids."

"What do you mean?" He'd been serious? Why wouldn't Randy want children? She glanced at him. There wasn't a hint of joking on his face.

"Forget it," he said. Then he turned his attention to the roof. "I'm surprised you don't have the top down."

"I thought it might distract the puppy on the way home."

"Ah. Makes sense."

She wanted to probe about the kids thing, but she didn't, and then Randy launched into the tale of Dorene and Lindy arguing over who got to change the baby, and she couldn't stop laughing.

"Austin was practically spitting fire at me when I left.

He'll get over it. I mean, a guy can only take so much in two days, and I hit my limit."

"Yeah, how are you doing? I mean, it's been a big upheaval for you."

"I'm handling it." His jaw tightened, and he stared out the window.

Was he, though? She hoped he wasn't too stressed out. He didn't seem to want to talk about it, so she let it drop.

After a while the training center came into view. She found a parking spot and inhaled deeply for a moment before getting out.

*God, I want this to go right. I want this puppy to help someone. Whatever I can do to train it, please guide me.*

"You okay?" Randy appeared at her side.

"Fine." She gave him her brightest smile, and they joined several families crossing the parking lot to the front entrance. But she wasn't okay. She usually had a rock-solid confidence in her plans, but right now, she wasn't sure she was up to the task.

Was it lack of faith? In God? In herself?

What if the dog didn't like her? Ned still seemed to tolerate her more than love her, but that dog sure adored Randy. Couldn't get enough of him, in fact.

Her theory on Ned being more comfortable around men was the most logical explanation for it. But what if it was her? What if the puppy didn't bond with her, either?

She couldn't stand the thought of failing to train the puppy correctly. It would be a waste of more than a year of her life, and it would be a waste of a potential service dog.

Was she up for this?

Randy opened the door for her, and she hurried inside.

When a child jostled her in the hall, he took her elbow to steady her.

"You okay?" he asked.

She nodded. They all took seats in the main training area, and Molly addressed them, talking about the puppies they were getting and how important it was to support each other. Since most of the puppy raisers lived more than an hour away, Molly had set up weekly online meetings for them to discuss problems and progress with each other. She'd also handed out instructions for them.

"Remember, the first couple of weeks should be fun, with lots of cuddles, and you can start training them basics and rewarding them for good behavior right away…" Molly continued until she finished going over the instructions. "When I call your name, Brian here will take you to your new puppy to get acquainted. Liz Saunders? Oh, there you are…"

"You nervous?" Randy whispered. He'd been sitting quietly next to her on a folding chair, and even in her nervousness, she hadn't forgotten he was there. In fact, seeing the couples and families all waiting to get their puppies made her thankful to have Randy for moral support.

"Yeah, I'm a little nervous." Or a lot.

"You'll be great. Look how amazing Ned is."

"Yeah, well, he came that way. And he doesn't feel the same about me as he does you." She hoped she didn't sound peevish. She'd meant it in a teasing way.

"What are you talking about? He loves you."

"I get the feeling he'd rather be somewhere else sometimes." Like with Randy.

"Maybe he's just used to being needed."

Huh, why hadn't she thought of that? It made sense.

Ned had spent his entire life with a purpose. He might not have been ready to retire.

Molly called two more names, and Hannah fidgeted in her seat. Would the dog be a Labrador? Or a golden retriever? Or another breed? Her palms grew sweaty.

"This place isn't what I expected." Randy craned his neck to look around.

"What did you expect?"

He shrugged. "I don't know. Not this."

"Hannah Carr." Molly waved her up there.

"That's me." She rose, her chest thumping. Randy stood, too.

"Mind if I join you?" he asked. "Or should I wait here?"

She'd wanted to meet the puppy with no distractions. But right now, in this moment, she wanted Randy with her. "Come with me."

Together, they followed Brian to the adjacent indoor play area where puppies and their raisers were getting acquainted. She and Randy went inside the enclosure.

"Wait right here, and I'll bring him out." Brian lifted his finger, then loped away.

Her mouth went dry. And she clasped her hands so tightly her knuckles grew white.

"Hey," Randy said, putting his arm around her shoulders and squeezing. "It's going to be fine."

She nodded, hoping he was right. And then Brian approached, holding a wiggly, plump golden retriever puppy.

"This is Barley." He set the puppy down in front of her, and tears formed in her eyes. Sniffing, she crouched to let him smell her hand before petting him. All her fears and worries vanished as the puppy leaped into her arms, almost knocking her backward.

She laughed. "Oh, he's the cutest thing."

Randy crouched next to her and let Barley sniff his hand, too, before petting him.

"I don't think I've ever seen a fluffier pup." He grinned at the furball.

The puppy licked her face, then hopped out of her arms and ran in a circle around them. When he shifted to run away, Randy extended his arm and corralled the dog back. "Oh, no, you don't." Then he met her eyes. "Do you have a leash?"

"Yes. It's in my tote." Still sitting next to the chairs they'd abandoned moments ago. She started to push herself up, but he held up a palm.

"Let me. You two can get to know each other. Is it by the chairs?"

"Yes." Having Randy here had been exactly what she'd needed. And she hadn't even known it.

Barley pounced on a toy, and she laughed. He was an energetic little thing, that was for sure. *Thank You, Lord. Thank You for this opportunity.*

She picked Barley up and hugged him to her. "You and I have a lot of work to do, little guy."

And she couldn't wait to get started.

The next morning Randy rode his horse past the barns to check for Hannah's Jeep. No sign of it. His spirits sank. He didn't know why he was so keyed up for her to get there. It wasn't as if he had any burning questions for her. He just wanted to know how the first night with Barley had gone. He'd been surprised at how nervous she'd seemed before she met the dog.

Hannah had never struck him as the nervous type.

Plus, her comment about Ned liking him more than

her kept picking at him. If she only knew why Ned preferred him…

Whether the dog knew it or not, Ned seemed to be letting Randy know when his body was out of whack. At least, he assumed that was what Ned was doing. Maybe the dog really did like him more. Who knew? He wasn't an expert.

Randy patted the horse's neck and stared at the drive. Waited a minute. And sighed. Still no sign of her.

Thankfully, AJ had slept better last night. He'd woken twice, and each time Randy fed him a bottle and he'd fallen back to sleep in no time. This morning, while Austin got dressed, Randy had changed the baby and gotten a bottle ready. Then, when Austin came downstairs, he'd handed him AJ and the bottle and made himself a strong cup of coffee.

Naturally, his brother had barked out a list of things to do around the ranch until Randy decided even the coffee wasn't worth it. He'd slipped Austin a handwritten list of deliveries to check on, told him to text if he needed anything and he'd left.

That had been an hour ago. Hannah was supposed to be here any minute so Austin could leave to open the store. Thankfully, his brother had helped him out at Watkins Outfitters many times in the past and knew what to do.

Randy yawned and debated his next move. Check on the cow who'd been limping or wait here another minute?

A vehicle rumbled up the drive. But it wasn't Hannah's Jeep parking next to Austin's truck. It was…Miss Patty?

She got out of the car and opened the passenger door. Then she took out a large bag, shut the door and made her way up to the house.

What was her mom doing here? Had something happened to Hannah? He rode to the porch, dismounted and tied the horse to the rail. Took the steps two at a time and made his way to the kitchen.

"Oh, hi, Randy." Miss Patty beamed. "Hannah wanted to spend the day getting to know Barley. She's a worrywart about getting it right with the puppy, so I told her I'd take care of our sweet little AJ today."

"I'd better take off." Austin came into the room, kissing her cheek. "Thanks a million. Randy should be done by—when do you think you'll be done, Randy?"

"Around three." He forced himself to act normal. It was ridiculous to be this disappointed that Hannah wasn't here.

"If you need anything," Austin said, "text or call either one of us."

"Oh, don't worry about me, boys." She waved them off. "It's just a baby. We'll get along fine, won't we, sweetheart." She picked up AJ, held him close and smiled down at him. The woman should be awarded Grandma of the Year. And this wasn't even her grandkid.

"Thanks again." Austin hobbled his way out the door and, a few minutes later, the truck engine roared to life.

"Are you sure you don't mind?" Randy asked.

"Honey, I never pass up a chance to hold a baby. You see how small he is now? Blink twice and he'll be over six feet tall. You kids grow up too quick. So, no, I don't mind. Not at all."

He stood there a moment, unsure if he should leave or not.

"I'm sure all this drama has put a damper on your house plans." Miss Patty carried the baby over to the kitchen counter and poured herself a cup of coffee. "Hannah mentioned how close you were to finishing the painting. I think she enjoyed helping you out."

He perked up at the thought. "I appreciated her help. It's a big job for one person."

"Yes. Big house for one person, too." Her innocent eyes didn't fool him. She had matchmaker written all over her. But unlike the church ladies who'd circled him and Austin yesterday, he didn't mind it on her. "Your mama would be proud of you. I always liked her. Sheryl and I had a lot in common. We both married stubborn ranchers, and neither of us would have changed it for the world. She had a soft touch with horses. That's where we differed. I've never been much of a rider. Anyway, I wish she could see her grandbaby."

He didn't think about his mother much. Didn't remember much about her, either. His memories were vague, but then, he'd been young when she'd died.

"I wish she could, too."

"If you and Austin need anything, Frank and I are always here for you. I hope you know that."

He realized it was true. It had been true since Dad died. He and Austin had relied on the Carrs many times over the years.

"We know it. We appreciate it." The words weren't adequate. He didn't know what to say, how to show his gratitude. "Especially all the baked goods."

She laughed. "I'll keep them coming, honey."

"And I'll keep eating them." He grinned. "I'd better get back out there."

"Okay, you have fun."

Fun? He had to locate a cow who'd shown signs of a hoof problem yesterday and possibly give her a shot of antibiotics. He wouldn't call that fun.

Randy turned to leave, then paused. "Did Hannah tell you how Barley is doing?"

"He's doing great. Whimpered a bit last night, but that's normal. He'll get used to his new home."

"What about Ned? Does he like the pup?"

"I don't know. I didn't even think to ask. Want me to find out?"

"That's okay. It's not a big deal."

"I'm sure she wouldn't mind if you stopped over there later. You could see for yourself."

"I won't bother her. I'll see her tomorrow, anyhow. Unless…she is coming tomorrow, isn't she?"

"She'll be here." Miss Patty smiled. "She'll be here."

Caring for AJ and watching a new puppy was turning out to be more challenging than Hannah had anticipated. Of course, it was only Tuesday, her first day of this arrangement. Any minute now Randy would come through the door, and she'd be able to take Ned and out-of-control Barley home. She couldn't wait.

Yesterday, Austin had been fine with her asking her mom to babysit. Naturally, she'd run it by him first. She'd known she'd regret it if she didn't spend Barley's first twenty-four hours completely devoted to him.

AJ smacked his lips together twice, let out a soft sigh and nestled deeper in Hannah's arms. He'd fallen asleep ten minutes ago, and although the babe had napped in the morning, it was the first time all day she'd been able to relax, mainly because Barley had finally passed out on the floor in a splotch of sunlight. Ned lay sleeping near her feet.

Ned had been somewhat out of sorts all day. He didn't seem to know if he should be watching the puppy or the baby or Hannah herself. The poor guy was as tired as the rest of them.

Steps outside alerted her that reinforcements had arrived. Finally.

She really needed to start making a list of potential nannies for Austin to hire. Later, though. After she took the dogs home and spent some one-on-one training time with Barley.

Just the thought of working with him made her want to crawl into bed and sleep for hours. It had been an absolutely exhausting day. And she'd promised her nieces and nephews they could come over and play with the puppy tomorrow night. If tomorrow was anything like today, she didn't know if she could handle it.

"Hey." Randy appeared in the archway to the living room and immediately cringed. "Sorry, I didn't realize he was asleep."

She shifted to stand and gently settled AJ into the baby seat nearby. He moved a little but didn't wake up. Then she pressed her hands into her lower back.

"How's everything on the ranch?" She crossed the room to gather her tote and to find Barley's leash. Ned woke up and ambled over to Randy.

"Good." He stroked Ned's fur. "I worked with Luke moving some cattle today, and it went more smoothly than last week."

"I'm glad," she said. "AJ's doing great, too. He had a nap this morning, and he fell asleep around three. He's so alert."

"Yeah, he's bright." He cocked his head to the side. "You don't happen to have any numbers for babysitters, do you? You mentioned knowing the teens in the area…"

"I do." Scrolling through her contacts, she found her

top three candidates and texted their information to Randy. "All three of them are good with children. They help at the church's nursery."

"If I can get a sitter for tonight, I'm heading over to the house to keep painting. I wish Austin was off those crutches already."

"Yeah, I do, too. I'm sure he wishes it more than we do." She snapped the leash on Barley's collar, waking him up, then slung her purse over her shoulder. "Well, I should probably head out."

"How's Barley doing? Is he settling in okay?" Randy leaned against the wall, one ankle crossed over the other. The puppy stretched out his legs and ambled to him, wagging his tail the entire way.

She sighed. "Well, he had three accidents on your hardwood floor today, so he could be doing better. Don't worry. I cleaned them all up."

"Accidents happen." His lips twitched and eyes danced. "Does Ned like him?"

"I think so. I do think it's been a little chaotic for the old boy being around a hyper puppy and a baby. He makes his rounds to me then Barley. Then he sniffs the baby and starts the rotation all over again."

"Aw, he needs a break, doesn't he?" Randy bent to scratch behind Ned's ears. The dog's tongue lolled as he basked in the attention. "He can paint with me tonight if you think he needs a break from Barley. That is, if I can find a sitter."

She considered for a moment. It would give her a chance to work with Barley one-on-one, and there was no mistaking Ned's devotion to Randy. But she also wanted him to bond with her.

*Don't be selfish. Ned's needs come first.*

"Yeah, he'd love it." She really had to get a handle on this insecurity about Ned. He was a dog. He could like who he wanted. He didn't owe her anything.

"Is it okay if I pick him up later?" Randy asked. She nodded. He swooped Barley into his arms and asked him about his day as he rubbed his fur. The puppy ate up the attention, wiggling ecstatically. Ned barked twice.

And AJ began to cry.

*Great.* Hannah closed her eyes briefly, dropped the leash and headed to the baby. Randy set Barley down, and the puppy raced over to lick AJ's face.

"No lick." Hannah blocked him with her arm as she lifted the baby into her arms.

"Here, I'll take him." Randy stood next to her, his forearm brushing her hand as he took a firm hold of the baby. Then he cradled him to his chest and looked down at him with affection.

Hannah's breath caught at the picture they made.

A strong man holding a baby.

Then she blinked her way out of it and found the pacifier. AJ had calmed by then, and he stared up at his uncle's face as if it were the most fascinating thing in the world.

Hannah didn't blame him. It was fascinating.

"Uh, if you have everything under control here, I'll let myself out." She felt hot all of a sudden. Flustered. She gathered her purse, the tote and the dogs. Then she felt a warm, moist tongue on the back of her hand. Ned stared up at her.

Maybe he was starting to love her, too.

She petted him.

"I'll pick Ned up after supper if I can find a sitter." He followed her to the door. AJ was content in his arms. "I'll text you."

"Sounds good." She touched AJ's cheek and gave the baby a smile before letting herself out.

Once she and the dogs were settled in the Jeep and she was half a mile down the road, the tension in her neck started to ease.

She was getting too caught up with Randy Watkins. And seeing him holding a baby so tenderly didn't help.

Sure, she'd thought of him as a brother for most of her life. But he wasn't her brother, and she didn't see him that way anymore. Hadn't for a while.

Was it so terrible to think of him as a man?

She swallowed, rolling down the window and relishing the sensation of the air whipping through her hair. Sunny afternoon. Wyoming summer in bloom.

The only reason she was thinking about Randy was due to the fact she'd been helping him out, spending time with him. When Austin got off the crutches and they hired a nanny, everything would go back to normal. And she wouldn't have these inconvenient feelings anymore.

Did Randy have them for her?

She didn't know. And she didn't want to think about it.

Because if she started letting her heart open up to him, and he told her she was too much, it would hurt far worse than hearing it from Shawn.

Maybe if Randy showed her some sign he had stronger feelings for her she could take a chance. Or maybe not. She just didn't know. And she wasn't sure she wanted to find out.

Shawn had been right about one thing—her expectations were high. Too high. And the only thing they'd gotten her so far was years of being single. She didn't see that changing anytime soon.

# *Chapter Six*

One benefit of AJ coming into their lives? All the frozen casseroles from the local ladies. Randy pulled out a container marked Chicken Enchiladas from the freezer Wednesday evening. The foil had directions written in Sharpie to preheat the oven and bake for an hour. He was getting spoiled with all these precooked, delicious meals. Austin was a fan of enchiladas, too, and Randy wanted him in a good mood tonight.

It was time to ask the questions that had been on his mind since the baby arrived.

He needed to know the truth about AJ's mom.

The longer they went without talking about it, the more Randy wondered if his brother was the man he'd always believed him to be.

He turned on the oven and adjusted the temperature, then popped the frozen container into the oven. AJ was waving a small stuffed cow around, trying to shove it in his mouth as he kicked in the bouncy chair.

Randy washed his hands before taking a seat at the kitchen table. He probably should have stayed home last night and had this conversation, but a restless energy had summoned a tornado inside him, and the only way to relieve it had been to go to the house and paint. He'd been thankful one of the teens Hannah had suggested had been free to babysit AJ for a few hours. It had given Austin a much-needed break, too.

What surprised Randy the most about painting last night, though, was how much he'd liked having Ned around. The dog helped calm him and, for whatever reason, made him feel safe. Not against an intruder or anything like that. More with his health. Like if he were to collapse, the dog would be there to keep him company.

Sometimes he worried about dying alone.

He'd been careful not to linger at Hannah's last night when he picked up Ned. She'd been working with Barley, using a clicker and giving him a treat for going into his crate. She said it was important for him to enjoy his kennel so he'd have a place to feel safe. Plus, dogs didn't like to soil their beds, so it helped with potty training at night. Made sense.

Then, later when he'd dropped Ned off, he hadn't even entered her apartment. Just thanked her and handed her the leash, staring at her too long in the process.

Even when they weren't together, he thought about her. He kept going back to the phone conversation he'd overheard last Friday when she'd jokingly mentioned being seated with her brothers at Tess's wedding. Felt like a lifetime ago. The strange thing was, he kept considering asking her to be his date to the wedding. He didn't need a date, though, and neither did she, since they were both in the wedding party.

The screen door clanged, and the unmistakable clop of the crutch grew closer.

"What a day." Austin took a seat kitty-corner to him

and bent down to smile at AJ. "Hey, there, buddy, how are you? You like that cow? Tastes pretty good, doesn't it?"

"Did the waders come in?" Randy asked. Every day he thought of all the things he needed to check at the store when he got a free minute. He should have stopped in last night before painting, but he'd been too keyed up.

"Half the shipment did. The other half won't be here until Friday." Austin's face looked less haggard lately. "How's the red tag 14 doing? Did you treat the pink eye? Don't want it spreading to the rest of the herd."

"Yep. Got her into the squeeze shoot and Luke sprayed the medication while I prepared the eye patch. It took us a while, but she stayed calm. We talked to her and petted her a lot."

"Good. Makes it easier to treat them when they trust you."

He'd grown up with cattle and hadn't spent much time thinking about the trust factor. He supposed it was true. With people, too.

"One of the bulls is determined to take out part of the fence bordering one of the pastures," Randy said. "We're going out there tomorrow to reinforce it."

"The two new bulls are still figuring out where they stand with the older boys." Austin chuckled. "They'll all be a lot happier next month when they move to the pasture with the cows."

"That they will." Time to ease his way into the conversation he could no longer put off having. "It's been a wild couple of weeks, huh?"

"Yeah." Austin nodded. "Without your help and Hannah's…" He shook his head, sighing. "Thanks. I know this has all been happening at the worst possible time. When everything settles down, I'll help you with the house. And I hate to lean on Hannah, but I don't even know where to start with trying to hire a nanny."

"She doesn't mind." He knew deep down it was true. Hannah seemed to thrive on helping people.

"I have a whole new respect for her and for you." Austin leaned back and stared at him. "Your store is impressive. It's organized. Well-stocked. I've had people from other states come in to get items they can't find anywhere else. They all complimented it."

"They ever hear of online shopping?" He tucked away Austin's words even as they filled him with pride.

"I think they like the adventure of coming in person."

"Well, I've got to hand it to you, too. The ranch is in the best shape I've ever seen it. The herd's growing, and it's because of your hard work."

"I try," he said softly. "I think of Dad and what he'd want. Makes it easier."

Randy's spirits fell. What would Dad think of his choices?

It didn't matter at this point. Dad was gone.

"Austin, we've lived under the same roof my entire life. You're my best friend." He fought to find the right words. "I need to know. Need to hear it from you. Why didn't you tell me you had a girlfriend?"

Austin straightened, clearly chewing on a thought.

"I'm having a hard time trying to reconcile the man I know with one who didn't take responsibility for his own baby." Randy kept his voice even, trying his best not to sound harsh and judgmental. "Will you explain?"

He waited for a gruff *I don't owe you an explanation.* But it didn't come.

"You have the right to know." Austin seemed to deflate. "But only if you promise me it never leaves this room. It's my business. No one else's. Do you agree?"

"Agree."

"Camila wasn't my girlfriend."

His stomach dropped. Had Austin had a one-night stand?

"Remember the summer after Dad died?" Austin waited for him to nod. "We hired Bo, and not long after, I took off for a long weekend in September. I was twenty-one, and my life kind of just hit me. I told you I was going to Alabama to see Ricky. I didn't go to Alabama. I didn't see Ricky."

Ricky had been one of Austin's childhood friends who'd moved to Alabama their sophomore year of high school.

"Where'd you go?"

"San Antonio, Texas. It's where Mom and Dad met. I wanted to catch a spark of them. But I didn't. And I was mad. Furious at God for taking them. I turned my back on Him. In fact, I ended up at a dive bar where I proceeded to drink myself into a stupor. I wasn't sure I was coming back to Wyoming. I wasn't really sure if I wanted to be alive anymore. I knew I could never fill Dad's shoes. Since Bo was back here, I knew you'd be in good hands. I was lost, Randy. Lost."

Randy had no idea Austin had gone through all that.

"The hour got late. I'd been drinking for hours. I didn't notice the people around me or the new arrivals. A guy started yelling at the bartender. Two other guys were with him. I barely registered them. The place started clearing out. Two shots were fired, and I just sat there, stunned, in a drunken fog. But someone grabbed my arm, hauled me to my feet and told me to follow her. I kept stumbling, and at one point, she hauled me as best as she could on her shoulders and practically carried me through the kitchen and out the back entrance. We didn't stop moving until we got to her car. She drove me to her apartment."

Randy sat there trying to take it all in, but so many questions remained.

"I crashed on her couch, passed out. A few hours later, I woke up with a brutal headache. She was sitting across from me, watching me. It all came back. I was so ashamed. I'd been incapable of helping myself or anyone else back at the bar. She told me three people were shot after we got out of there. I stumbled to her bathroom and threw up."

Randy didn't move. He'd never known. And he could see in Austin's face and hear in his voice how much shame he carried over the event.

"I asked her why she'd bothered to help me. I mean, she saved me. And you know what she said?"

Randy shook his head.

"She told me she'd been watching me for a while. That I looked lost. Then she said something I'll never forget."

"What?"

"She told me that morning she'd been reading her Bible. And she'd been struck by Jesus's words about having compassion on the crowds because they were like sheep without a shepherd. When she saw me sitting there, I reminded her of one of those sheep. She said she knew God had sent her there to help me."

"She knew you'd be there?"

"No, Randy. You're missing the point. God used her to save me. It was a defining moment in my life."

"Oh."

"She'd been trying to find her brother. No one had

seen him for a week. Camila's home life was messed up. Real messed up. She joined the military the day after she turned eighteen. Cut ties with her abusive dad. The only family left was her brother, and he'd gotten into trouble with the law. About a year after I met her, he died in a drug deal gone wrong. But Camila, man, she was strong. Little slip of a thing. But she was strong inside. I told her if there was anything—anything—I could ever do for her, I would do it."

Randy still wasn't grasping all the details, but he saw Austin through new eyes. "Did you fall in love? How does this tie in with AJ?"

"We were friends." Austin shook his head. "I'd visit every six months or so if she was in the States, and we'd catch up. Nothing romantic. Then last year she got involved with a guy she shouldn't have. Things went south real quick, but not before she found out she was pregnant. He threatened her, things escalated, and he beat her up, so she called me. Explained the situation. Didn't want the abuser anywhere near the baby."

Randy's head was spinning in fifty directions.

"I told her to put my name on the birth certificate. And I promised her I would raise the baby as my own if anything happened to her. She had no one close she could trust, and the last thing she ever wanted was for a child of hers to be raised by an abusive jerk."

"AJ's not yours." Randy slumped in his chair, blown away.

"I would have done anything for her. She saved my life when I needed it the most. If she hadn't been there… I don't know. I was in bad shape."

"You're raising another man's child as your own."

"I'm raising Camila's son as my own. There's a difference." Austin leveled an unblinking stare at him. "My name is on the birth certificate. I'll be the only daddy he knows. He's my son. Do you think I'd ever allow some monster who beats women near him? It'll never happen. And you can be sure AJ will know exactly how wonderful his mama was. Understand?"

Randy nodded.

"All right, then. As long as we're on the same page." Austin steepled his fingers. "Does this change how you feel about him?"

"No." It didn't, either. He'd fallen for the baby, head over heels.

"Good." The muscle in Austin's cheek flexed. "Does it change how you feel about me?"

Did it? Randy considered for a moment before answering. "Yes, it does."

Austin's face fell.

"For days I've been thinking the worst about you, trying to defend your actions in my mind, but hearing this? I feel like a fool. I should have known you wouldn't shirk your duties. You'd never turn your back on your child."

Austin's mouth dropped open. "But the drinking, the hopelessness… I actually thought about ending it all. Leaving you with Bo. It felt so overwhelming—running the ranch, figuring it all out without Dad."

Randy shrugged. "Understandable. It was a rough summer. We both know it."

They sat with their thoughts for a while.

"So you never dated her? Camila?"

A hint of a smile played on Austin's lips as he shook his head. "Nope. I admired her, though. I'm pretty tore up she died. I always looked forward to seeing her when I could. She was a special person."

"If you could do it over, would you have tried?"

"Dating her?" His face scrunched in confusion. "No. I told you. It wasn't like that with us. Besides, I don't see myself ever getting married."

Usually, this was the part where Randy announced he wasn't, either.

But being around Hannah was confusing him.

And that was a problem. Because confused or not, his heart condition wasn't getting any better.

Maybe he needed to man up and call the doctor soon. Find out how much the disease had progressed. Find out if he had any future—with or without Hannah.

"These are all the people I could think of who might be interested in watching AJ full-time for you." Hannah handed Austin the sheet of paper when she arrived at the ranch Thursday morning before he left to take care of Watkins Outfitters.

He scanned the paper as he leaned against one of the crutches. "Thanks, Hannah. I'll start calling them."

She still held Barley's leash. He was nosing around AJ's bouncy seat. She kept him far enough away that he couldn't lick the poor baby.

The little fluffball better not have an accident right now.

Barley still seemed confused as to what to do when she took him out every couple of hours. Take this morning. She'd led both him and Ned to the common grassy area outside her apartment. Ned did his business while Barley scampered around. She'd kept him out there for twenty minutes. But did he go? No. Then, the minute they went back into the apartment, he'd piddled on the carpet.

It had not been a good morning.

Austin had a funny look on his face.

"What's wrong?" she asked.

"Well, Leslie Brohan's dating one of Mac's cowboys, and rumor has it she's getting bumped up to assistant manager at the feedstore. So I probably can cross her off the list."

"Oh." How had Hannah not heard about this?

"And Sami started bartending at night over at The Pit. I could call her but…"

"Yeah, she's out." Hannah looked over his shoulder to scan the list. "That still leaves Bianca and Janelle."

He glanced up at her with pursed lips.

"What?" she asked. "You don't like them?"

"I didn't say that." He sighed. "I just don't know how good they are with kids."

Hannah worried about that herself. Her top contender—Leslie—would likely want the benefits that came along with a promotion at the feedstore. So much for hoping the list would yield a nanny.

Barley seemed to be searching for something.

"Will you excuse me a minute? I need to take him out."

"Go ahead." He waved her off, staring at the paper.

She called Barley by name and tugged on the leash for him to get moving. She never missed a chance to work on him with name recognition, and he was getting there. Dear Ned trotted beside her through the door, down the porch steps and out to the lawn where Randy was striding toward them.

Her breath caught in her throat. Probably due to him moving so purposefully toward her in full cowboy gear. Jeans, short-sleeved shirt showing off his muscles, cowboy hat and boots. His face was tanned from the sun.

He looked like the kind of guy who could sling you over his shoulder and carry you out of a burning building.

She was tempted to fan herself. "You're getting through those ranch chores in record time there, cowboy."

"Don't I wish." His lazy grin made her tummy do a flip. "I'm painting again tonight."

Was he going to ask her to help? She wanted to. She missed their time together.

But yesterday she'd canceled having her nieces and nephews over and promised to let them meet the puppy tonight. Her brother Michael and sister-in-law Leann were bringing Sunni and Cam over around four thirty, and her brother David and sister-in-law Kelli were dropping off Rachel, Bobby and Owen after supper.

She'd had to split their times up because five kids at once would be too much for Barley to handle. Too much for her right now, as well.

"I was wondering if I could borrow Ned again?" Randy tilted his head. "He's good company."

Disappointment slapped her. He wanted Ned to keep him company? Not her?

"Of course." She tried to sound chipper but was pretty sure she failed.

"Is he supposed to be eating that?" Barley was chomping the head of a dandelion.

"No! Barley, stop. No." She pulled him away and attempted to get the flower out of his mouth, but he swallowed it before she could. Were dandelions poisonous? And had he even gone to the bathroom?

She'd better get him inside and do a quick internet search on dandelions and dogs.

"Looks like your hands are full. Ned can hang out with me around the ranch for a while if you'd like."

One less thing she'd have to think about. "Ned would love it. He's not sure what to do with this one." She pointed to Barley, rolling in the grass. "Come, Barley."

"Is Austin still in there?"

"Yes. We're going over the list of potential nannies."

He nodded and they made their way back inside, where Austin was preparing to leave. Randy stopped him. "Do me a favor and print off the list of receipts for the past three days, will you?"

"Sure," Austin asked. "Anything else?"

"Can you bring home these lures?" Randy pulled a crumpled paper out of his pocket and handed it to his brother.

"Why? You planning on fishing or something?"

"It's been two weeks since I posted a video. These are the ones I planned on doing next." They continued to chatter as they went out the door with Ned, leaving Hannah alone with Barley and AJ.

No goodbyes.

And the nanny list abandoned on the table.

Ignored and forgotten. Much like her.

Hannah unclipped the leash, then took AJ out of the bouncy seat. "Looks like it's just the three of us today. Will you help me with Barley, little buddy?"

The baby cooed, and she sat at the table with him on her lap, pulled out her phone and did a search to find out if dandelions were poisonous to dogs. Thankfully, they were not.

Something told her it was going to be a long day...

Several hours later, Hannah plunked down on the couch as frazzled as she could ever remember being. Barley had piddled twice on the floor, both mere minutes after she'd taken him outside. Then AJ had gotten cranky, and while she was trying to calm him down by gently bouncing him, the puppy had torn up a new diaper, which had taken forever to clean up.

After the baby finally fell asleep, Barley saw a spider and started barking and pouncing at it, which woke AJ. The crying had begun all over again.

At that point, she'd been ready to cry herself.

And to top it all off, she'd taken it upon herself to call all four women on the list, and not one of them was interested in babysitting full-time.

Austin and Randy had to hire a nanny. Soon.

She couldn't keep up with this. Barley needed attention and discipline, Ned needed consistency, and AJ needed a full-time caregiver. This situation wasn't sustainable.

Would it be wrong to ask Hannah to help him paint tonight?

After supper Randy knocked on Hannah's apartment door. He'd hired a teen to help Austin with AJ for a few hours. With two rooms left to paint, Randy was beginning to feel more hopeful about moving in at the end of the month. He still needed to work on the landscaping, but he could do that later this summer. If he could cross off a few more items on his list this weekend, he'd be on track.

The door opened to Hannah. Her cheeks were flushed. The shouts of small children made him stretch his neck to see beyond her. One of David's kids jumped up and down and squealed as Barley chased him. The oldest of the bunch, Rachel, scolded him. "Bobby, don't do that. You're making him hyper."

"He likes it," Bobby said. "Owen, don't lift him like that—"

Hannah spun around and returned to the kids. "Okay, what did we talk about?"

All three of them dropped their chins.

"We have to sit down and wait for Barley to come to us." Rachel flashed a glare at one of the boys. Randy went inside, closed the door and stood near the edge of the room.

"That's right." Hannah nodded. "Bobby, why do we have that rule?"

"Cuz puppies get wild, and we don't want him to get too rough. He's got to learn how to be a good dog so he can help someone in a wheelchair."

Hannah smiled at him and, bending down, put her hand on his shoulder. "Very good. But he might help someone who *can* walk. Maybe the person is blind. Or has autism or diabetes. We don't know."

Ned loped over to Randy and sat next to him, surveying the scene.

"Hi, Mr. Randy," Rachel said, skipping over. He guessed she was about eight years old, but he wasn't great at guessing ages. "How many minnows do you have at your store?"

"I reckon I have two million, six hundred and fifty-three thousand." He always got a kick out of her questions when she came into the store with her dad. "Give or take a few."

"That many?" She shifted her weight to one hip and gave him a skeptical look. "Do you count them every night?"

"Every night." He winked.

Owen, the youngest, yawned, rubbing his eyes, and

Hannah picked him up and settled him on her hip. "Ned's going to help Mr. Randy paint his new house. Isn't that nice?"

"Dogs can't paint." Bobby shook his head.

"He'll be supervising." Hannah's dancing eyes met Randy's gaze, and he tamped down the laughter welling up. Kids. He never knew what would come out of their mouths.

"Barley!" Rachel raced away from him. "No, you can't eat that!"

"I'd better take care of this." Hannah jerked her thumb to the kitchen where the puppy had disappeared to. She set Owen back on his feet. "Ned's leash is on the entry table."

Right. He'd momentarily forgotten he was only there to pick up the dog. And Hannah clearly wasn't free to help him paint. Disappointment slid down his core.

"I could help you paint, Mr. Randy." Bobby flashed a grin with one bottom tooth missing.

"I'm sure you could, bud, but your aunt wouldn't be too happy with me if I took you away from Barley right now."

The kid nodded. "When I grow up, I'm going to work at your store. I'm gonna go fishing all the time."

"Sounds like a good plan, buddy." Tickled, he smiled at the boy. He'd forgotten what it was like to have someone look up to him. "I'll set aside a special lure for you the next time your dad stops by."

"Really?" His grin grew even wider. "I'm gonna catch me a big old bass with it."

"That's the idea." He ruffled Bobby's hair. "Well, I'd better get going. Have fun with the puppy."

Hannah returned with Barley. Rachel talked up a storm next to her.

"I'll drop him back off in a couple of hours," Randy said, attaching the leash to Ned's collar.

"Okay. Hope you get a lot done." Did he detect longing in her tone?

"Me, too. Have fun. See you guys later."

All three kids yelled goodbye to him as he turned to leave. Outside, his spirits dropped.

He liked those kids. Hannah was great with them. If things were different, he could see himself with a couple of munchkins, too. Taking them fishing. Roughhousing with them.

He held the truck door open for Ned and, once the dog was safely inside, shut it.

But things weren't different.

Not now, they weren't.

Could they be?

Tomorrow. He'd call the doctor tomorrow. But the thought filled him with dread. It would mean more tests. Medications that might not work. Side effects. Surgery wasn't off the table. Maybe even worse news.

He started up the truck and checked his mirrors to back out. He owed it to himself to find out. Even if he didn't like the results.

## Chapter Seven

"You have big weekend plans?" Hannah asked Randy Friday afternoon as Barley sniffed the floor near her feet.

"Nothing major," Randy said. He'd finished the chores early and was ready to relieve her of babysitting duties. "I'm helping Austin with the baby. I plan on ordering my appliances. I still have another room to paint, too. The cabinets were installed, so that's good. Two more weeks and I can move in."

He liked these moments with Hannah. As soon as she left, though, he was calling the doctor to set up an appointment.

"How does it look?" She had a dreamy expression. "White cabinets, right?"

"Yeah. Figure it would keep the space looking bright. It looks good." It looked better than good. Now that the construction was wrapping up, he was getting anxious to move in. He'd already asked the guys to set aside the Monday night before Sawyer's wedding to help him move. He didn't have much furniture at this point, so it shouldn't take long.

He supposed he should start shopping for a couch.

And chairs. And what about the other stuff he took for granted? Things like rugs and curtains?

His pulse began to race, and he closed his eyes, not wanting to think about everything he'd been putting off. A licking sensation made him open them. Whenever he got wound up, Ned seemed to be there to remind him to calm down.

Good old Ned.

"Well, I'd better go." She attached the leashes to the dogs' collars, gathered her purse and gave him a wave as she strolled away. "Let me know if you need anything."

"I will."

She gave him a slight smile and left. He waited until he heard the Jeep's engine roar before he dialed the doctor.

It rang three times and an automated voice answered, instructing him to press one. He obeyed and listened to the options. By the time press four came around, AJ was getting cranky. Randy propped the phone between his shoulder and ear, then bent to pick up the baby. He did a quick search for the pacifier and popped it in the baby's mouth.

The voice was on number seven at that point.

He growled. Waited for the automation to repeat. *C'mon, c'mon.*

The baby sucked on the pacifier and relaxed in Randy's arms. He absentmindedly caressed the boy's forehead as he waited to hear the correct option.

Six. He pressed it to make an appointment. No one answered, though, as instrumental music played.

Were they for real? It should not be this complicated to make an appointment. A minute ticked by. Should he continue holding? This felt like a big waste of time.

Three more minutes passed before the phone rang and someone picked up.

"I need to make an appointment."

"Name?"

He told her.

"Looks like it's been five years since you've been in."

Yeah, that was about right.

"Are you experiencing any symptoms?"

"Lately, my heart's been racing a lot."

The sound of the door opening made him freeze. Hannah came back in with Barley, still leashed, and froze. "Sorry, I didn't mean to bother you. I left my cell phone here."

He nodded, unwilling to say another word.

"Mr. Watkins?"

"Yeah," he said gruffly.

"Any other symptoms?"

"No." This call needed to end ASAP. "Sorry, I've got to go." He hung up.

Still sucking on the pacifier, AJ blinked up at him. His face felt like a furnace. He didn't dare look at Hannah. She'd gone to the other room, anyhow.

"Eh-eh. Come." She practically dragged the dog into the kitchen with her. Her normally sparkling eyes were clouded over, and there were two red splotches on her cheeks.

"What's wrong?" he asked.

She shook her head and propped on a smile. "Nothing. It's nothing."

This week had been hard on her. Watching AJ, training Barley, having the kids over. How did she do it all?

Once more he was struck by how much he and Austin had been relying on her without really thinking how it was affecting her.

"Why don't you take a break?" he asked, wanting to make all her problems disappear. "Come with me to Freeze Bucket for a shake."

"Ye-e-es." The word flowed out so dramatically, he suppressed a chortle. "Are you sure you can? Sounded like a serious conversation on the phone."

How much had she heard? "Oh, that? It was nothing. Let's get out of here. I'm going stir-crazy, and AJ has only left the house once since arriving."

"Want me to pack the diaper bag?" she asked.

"I can do it," he said. "Should I change him? Or is this outfit okay?"

"It's fine. I'll get his hat, though. Don't want the sun beating down on his adorable little head." She let go of Barley's leash and headed to the front of the house where the staircase was located.

Randy buckled the baby into the car seat. Barley wagged his tail as he sniffed the baby's head. AJ reached his hand out to touch the pup. The wiggly dog could barely contain his excitement.

After grabbing a few diapers and a bottle, Randy tossed them into the diaper bag, which was baby blue with elephants marching across it. He did not want to sling that ridiculous thing over his shoulder. Maybe he'd talk to Austin about getting a backpack.

Hannah returned and handed him the hat.

"Does this look strange?" he asked.

"What?"

He pointed to the bag.

She lunged for Barley's leash before he could run into the other room. "The diaper bag? No, it's so sweet. Look at all those adorable elephants."

"Sweet?" He cringed. "Adorable?"

Her laugh filled the room. "Don't look so disgusted. The single ladies will be flocking to you to see little AJ. The married ones, too. And the old ones. Basically, you're a babe magnet now."

He glared at her. Her lips twitched with laughter. Barley let out a sharp bark, then sat back, his tongue lolling.

Randy's cell phone rang. He set the baby down and answered it.

"We got cut off earlier, but I have an opening if you want it." The receptionist from the doctor's office was on the line. "The doctor can fit you in at three on the twenty-eighth. Would that work?"

"Yes." He had no idea if it would work or not, but he didn't care at this point. The last thing he needed was Hannah to overhear any more of this conversation. "See you then." He ended the call, picked up the car seat and gestured. "Shall we?"

She gave him a strange look, shrugged and led the way outside.

Dealing with the baby, carrying an *adorable* and *sweet* elephant diaper bag, trying to manage his heart condition and simultaneously fighting this temptation regarding Hannah?

He was destined to fail. One—or all—would crash at some point.

He'd deal with the aftermath when it happened. First, he was ordering the largest chocolate shake Freeze Bucket offered.

She needed this break.

Hannah stood next to Randy in front of the walk-up window at Freeze Bucket and waited for their shakes to be made. Ned stayed close to Randy, and Barley was tugging at his leash, trying to catch a butterfly with his teeth.

The puppy was going to be the end of her.

And it wasn't even his fault.

She only had tonight and tomorrow left to work with him before her first puppy-raiser online meeting with the other families. And she really didn't want to be the lone failure. This was important—training the dog was important—and she'd barely taught him anything this week.

It was her fault. The short sessions she spent with him each night weren't enough. And the training schedule she'd printed before school let out was collecting dust in her bedroom. All those fun sessions she'd designed to condition him to basic dog-training commands? Hadn't happened.

She'd envisioned easily teaching him to lure—basically following her hand with a treat—while using marker commands such as *free* and *yes*. In all her fantasies, she'd been smiling and happy while the dog quickly learned the commands.

The reality? She'd been tired and tense with Barley, and he'd barely learned a thing.

"Two chocolate shakes." A high school boy she recognized handed them the shakes.

She kept a firm grip on both dog leashes. Randy turned to find a picnic table. He carried AJ in the car seat as they strolled across the mowed lawn to a table with an umbrella. The sun was beating down, but the breeze kept it from being unbearable.

Once seated, they both shoved their straws into the shakes. She held hers up. "To surviving the week."

He touched his shake to hers. "To surviving."

They met each other's eyes and smiled. It gave her a sense of being in this together, a secret—their secret. And it hit her in the best possible way. She'd grown used to not getting noticed by the guys around here, and she hadn't cared. But that smile… Randy noticed her. And she liked it.

"I never realized a baby could cry so much and sleep so little." He took his first sip. A look of pure bliss crossed his face.

"I never realized a puppy could tear up the entire contents of a bathroom wastebasket through an entire apartment in thirty seconds flat." She took a drink. So sugary. So good.

"I threw three baby outfits away this week because they had so much doo-doo on them I couldn't face cleaning them."

"I went through an entire bottle of pet-odor carpet cleaner trying to clean up Barley's accidents in the living room."

"Every time AJ cried in the night, I wanted to strangle my brother for spraining his ankle."

"Every time Barley whimpered in the night, I wanted to strangle the author of the puppy-care guide I'd been advising people to use to train their puppies. The author is clearly stupid and knows nothing."

"I'm not good at this." He kept drinking the shake. She knew he meant taking care of AJ.

"I'm a terrible puppy raiser." She met his eyes. His twinkled. "He'll never make the cut."

As if to prove her point, Barley let out three sharp barks. He'd wound the leash around his two hind legs somehow, and he looked like a lassoed calf. Ned nudged the puppy's head. She let out a long sigh and untangled him, then handed him a chew toy from her purse.

"I think Barley needs a lot of work." She raised her eyebrows. "A. Lot. Of. Work."

They drank their shakes in easy silence. The peace of the sunny day slowly erased all her insecurities. AJ was napping. Ned was sitting near Randy, staring up at him like he was his hero. And Barley, thankfully, had sprawled out to chew on the toy.

This was as good as it could get at this point.

She glanced at Randy. "I underestimated how much time and energy I would need to watch and train the puppy. Mistakes were made."

"Boy, you can say that again. Every time I take care of AJ, mistakes are made." Randy shrugged. "We'll find someone else to babysit him. Don't worry."

Like who? Mom had called all her friends, and none of them had any fresh suggestions for nannies, unfortunately.

"Maybe one of the teens could watch him. At least for the summer. By then someone else might be available." She pushed the shake to the side. If she didn't slow down, she'd get a stomachache.

"I suppose." He didn't seem very enthused. "I just want him to be in good hands."

"I do, too." She craned her neck to check on him, still sleeping. "He's such a good baby. You're doing a great job with him. You got thrown into baby care without any experience, and look how amazing he's doing."

"I don't feel like I'm doing a good job."

"Yeah, well, maybe you're too hard on yourself. In the past two weeks, you took over the ranch, got the best person in Sunrise Bend to take care of the store—me—"

she wiggled her fingers near her face "—and when your brother showed up with a baby you didn't know about, you instantly took action and helped with the baby and the ranch, too. All this while you're trying to finish up your house."

"Put like that, I guess I'm pretty amazing." His lazy grin was smug.

She rolled her eyes. "Don't get too cocky, there, cowboy."

"You're pretty amazing, too, you know." His voice was low. "The puppy? He'll be fine. He's young. You're teaching him more than you realize every day."

Randy thought she was amazing? A sudden lump formed in her throat. All the pressure she'd been under evaporated.

"I pictured it to be more formal."

"What?" he asked.

"The training."

"Oh, now I get it." He gave her a knowing grin. "You had a lesson plan for him, didn't you? And if you weren't watching AJ, I'm guessing you'd have his entire day scheduled like at school."

"I did *not* have his entire day scheduled." Her cheeks burned. Actually, she had created a loose schedule for each week to get him on the fast track to being a service dog.

"Sure, you didn't."

"Maybe I made up a few training plans…" A woman in line caught her eye. "Hey, is that Cassie Berber? I haven't seen her in years. Mind if I go say hi?"

"Be my guest."

Good, because the conversation was starting to make her squirm. He made her sound like a rigid, type A person. Having to be up at the crack of dawn, doing drills with the puppy.

"Want to leave Barley with me?" He held out his hand. "I'm warning you, though, if that dog wakes up AJ, I'm letting go of the leash. If he runs to the mountains, so be it."

She chuckled and handed him the leash, brushing her fingers against his in the process. She hurried over to the window where Cassie stood.

"Well, hey, there, stranger." Hannah tapped her shoulder. The gorgeous brunette turned and, recognizing Hannah, gave her a wide smile.

"It's so good to see you." Cassie threw her arms around her and hugged her tightly. Hannah hugged her back.

"Are you visiting your mom?" Hannah asked. "How long are you going to be in town? We have to get together."

"I'm here for good. Well, for a long while, anyway." A sundae slid through the window, and Cassie grabbed it, dunking the spoon into the hot fudge. They moved to the lawn. "Mom needs help with Gramps."

Hannah's spirits faltered. "I'm sorry. I heard he's been slowing down."

"That's one way to put it." Cassie nodded and took a bite. "Last month we found out it was worse than we thought. Vascular dementia. Not real shocking, considering his heart disease, diabetes and high blood pressure. He's been getting confused more often."

"Again, I'm so sorry." Hannah touched Cassie's arm.

"Thank you. Mom and I don't want him going to a nursing home. He's—I'm sorry, I don't mean to get teared up, it's just, he's like a father to me—" Cassie fanned herself. "Anyway, I'm back. Mom works second shift.

She gets home around midnight, so it's not hard. I'm keeping an eye on him when she's gone. He sleeps half of the time."

Hannah took her hand and squeezed it. "If there's anything I can do, just say the word. Mom and I can bring meals, stay with him if your mom needs to get out—whatever."

"We're not at that point, yet, but when we get there, I'll take you up on it. What I really need is a job. You don't happen to have one of those in your back pocket, do you?"

Hannah gaped at her. "Actually, Cassie, I do happen to have a job in my back pocket. How do you feel about babies?"

"I love babies."

"Come on. There's someone you have to meet."

"I've got good news." Randy carried the car seat into the kitchen an hour later. AJ was cooing happily and kicking his tiny feet. "Austin?"

His brother's truck was out front, but Randy didn't see any sign of him. He set the car seat down and unstrapped the baby. Then he lifted him out, pulled his T-shirt down and carried him to the living room.

Austin came down the steps—without crutches. "This ankle's on the mend. Tomorrow morning, I'm back on the ranch. You can return to the store."

Yes! His life was back!

Thoughts of getting to the store early, stocking the displays, fiddling with the lures, enjoying a large cup of coffee all by his lonesome before any customers arrived was so exhilarating, his knees threatened to buckle.

"Are you sure?" Randy forced himself back to reality. "Is it too early to be bearing weight on it?"

"Nah." Austin limped slightly on his way to the couch. "Here, let me." He took AJ out of his arms, kissed the boy's forehead and cradled him to his chest. "I've been waiting all week to do that again. It's nice to be able to carry my boy."

If he had any lingering doubts about Austin's commitment to being a father, they were permanently laid to rest.

"Well, I have good news, too." Randy sat in the recliner, popping the footrest up, while Austin baby-talked to AJ.

"What is it?" Austin carefully sat on the couch, keeping a firm hold on the boy.

"Hannah and I took this little guy to the Freeze Bucket just now, and we ran into Cassie Berber. Remember her?"

He frowned. "Kind of."

"She's younger than us. Stacy's daughter."

"Oh, right. Haven't seen Chuck in a while."

"That's why Cassie's back. His health's getting worse. She's helping her mom take care of him."

Austin nodded.

"She needs a job. Might be interested in taking care of AJ for us."

"Really?" Hope lit his eyes. "What did you think of her?"

"I think she'd be great with the baby. I don't know what kind of hours she's looking for, but I told her to stop by tomorrow morning to talk to you. You can meet her and see how she is with the baby. Have you thought about what you want to pay someone?"

"Top dollar." Austin didn't bat an eye. "I've got the money. I'm saving Camila's life insurance for his college fund."

Randy hadn't even thought to ask about any of those details.

"If we hire her, you know what this means?" His brother smiled down at the baby.

"What?"

"Our lives go back to normal. Well, as normal as they can be with this little squirt around."

Normal. How he wanted his life to be normal. Randy sank deeper into the recliner.

Working at the store. Finishing up the house. Moving in. Getting through Sawyer and Tess's wedding. And then…the entire summer to himself. Fishing and chilling and sitting on the deck watching the world go by.

Yes. Normal sounded really good.

Hannah came to mind. He could see her as his date to the wedding. He'd invite her over to grill now and then. Let the dogs run around out back. Enjoy each other's company.

The joy faded. Taking her to the wedding would send the wrong message. And Hannah wouldn't be content with grilling now and then.

He'd seen her with kids. Seen her with the baby.

She'd want more. And she deserved it.

He sighed. Maybe the doctor would have good news for him.

*Sure, the doctor's going to take one look at you and declare your heart is healed. It doesn't work that way.*

No matter how much he fantasized about a normal life, it wasn't going to happen.

Misleading her wouldn't be fair. It wouldn't be right.

He wouldn't do that to her.

## Chapter Eight

❧

So this was what normal life was like.

Boring.

Hannah flopped onto her couch Monday afternoon. Ned and Barley were stretched out next to each other near the patio door, where sunlight fell in a long stripe. Her poor, tired guys.

On Saturday Austin had called to let her know she didn't need to babysit anymore. He'd hired Cassie on the spot. Hannah was glad. Hiring her had allowed them all to get back to their routines.

Randy had returned to the store, Austin had resumed ranching, and she'd finally started her summer vacation the way she'd imagined it. And all had been fine…until an hour ago. After two weeks of busy, busy, busy, she wasn't sure what to do with hours and hours of free time. She was tempted to stop by Watkins Outfitters. See how Randy was doing. Ask if he needed help painting. Maybe even chat with Joe Schlock.

She must be desperate.

It wasn't as though she'd been a lazy bum all day. She'd woken early, played with the dogs—Ned had actually seemed happy for once—packed away all the teaching supplies, cleaned her apartment, had two short training sessions with Barley that had gone better than she'd expected, made herself a healthy lunch, talked to Mom for twenty minutes on the phone and taken the dogs for a short walk.

She should probably be tired. She wasn't, though. A restless energy zipped through her veins, urging her to text Cassie to make sure AJ was okay or to call Tess to find out if she needed help with any wedding details, even though she'd talked to her yesterday and Tess hadn't mentioned anything.

Her nails caught her attention. They looked scraggly. Hopping up, she tried to remember if she had any clear polish left. She rarely wore colors since her nails tended to take a beating in the classroom.

A new bottle of clear polish sat in her bathroom drawer, so she filed her nails and swiped two coats on.

Now what?

Ned and Barley were still conked out. Her heart squeezed for the black Lab. Ned was such a trouper, but he seemed out of sorts. Like he was watching for someone or wanted to be somewhere else.

Could a dog be depressed?

Barley yawned. Wagging his tail, he ambled over to her, looking up with trusting eyes. Hannah got on the floor and petted him, hoping her nails were dry. "You're a good boy, aren't you? Only one accident today. How about we try no accidents tomorrow?"

He mouthed her hand, and she pulled it away, reaching to get a toy for him to chew instead.

Ned woke, too, took one look at her and changed positions, chin on his paws again. He let out a pathetic sigh and licked his chops. She checked her watch. Not quite four thirty.

"All right, fellas, it's time for a field trip. Let's go see Randy." At the sound of Randy's name, Ned's ears perked forward.

It told her everything she needed to know. The dog missed him.

She kind of did, too.

After leashing the dogs and taking Barley out for a potty break, she drove the short distance to Watkins Outfitters. Then she led both dogs through the front door of the store where Joe stood in front of the fishing rods.

"Hi, Joe. Buying new gear?" She gave the older man a smile.

"Well, Hannah, it's good to see you back." He gave her his full attention. "Will you be minding the store again?" His hope-filled eyes went straight to her heart. He was lonely, and she'd actually enjoyed talking to him the week she'd managed the store.

"No, I'm busy with these two rascals." She nodded to the dogs.

"Ah, there's Ned." Joe petted his head. "What's the young 'un's name?"

"Barley. I'm raising him for a year or so. Then he'll go on to train to be a service dog."

"You don't say?" Joe rubbed his chin. "It'll be hard letting him go. He sure is cute."

"He is, isn't he?" She wouldn't argue with that. "Is Randy around?"

"He's in the back." Joe yanked his thumb over his shoulder.

"I'll go find him. It was nice seeing you again."

She continued to the back and leaned her shoulder

against the doorjamb of the storeroom, where Randy was lifting a box onto a high shelf. "I see you're back in your natural habitat."

"Hey." A grin spread across his face. "You brought Ned." The dog got as close as the leash would allow, so she let go of it. Ned sat directly in front of Randy, staring up with his tongue out. "I missed you, boy." Randy glanced at her. "What brings you out here? I figured you'd be lounging all day, finally enjoying your summer vacation."

"I'm not much of a lounger." She nodded to Ned. "I think he misses you."

"You think?"

"Oh, yeah."

"Well, he's welcome here anytime. He's practically the store mascot. Everyone's been asking where he's been."

"That's sweet…" Barley was sniffing a box nearby.

"I'd love to have him around more."

"I don't know." No arguments came to mind. Sure, he was her dog, but wasn't part of being a dog owner doing what was best for him? Was it selfish that she wanted him to be with her all the time so she could bond with him? "He's my responsibility."

Randy shrugged. "The offer stands. I could pick him up on my way in. Would give you more time to work with Barley."

The idea tempted her. More than tempted her. Ned would love being with Randy. And she would be able to focus on Barley during the day. "Barley does need a lot more work. The first online meeting with the other puppy raisers was yesterday. Most of them were like me, struggling to potty-train and corral their pups, but there were a few who have already gotten their puppies to respond to several commands."

"Well, there you go."

"You wouldn't mind?"

"Of course not."

"Okay, then. I think it would be good for him. Only the mornings, though. I'll pick him up at lunchtime. If it's not going well after a week, I'll just keep him with me." She checked on Barley. He must not have found anything exciting in his sniffing, because he'd plunked down near her feet. "How's everything else going?"

"Great. I finished painting yesterday, and I haven't had to look at a cow since Friday." His face positively lit up. "The only negative was the church ladies dropping off another week's worth of casseroles yesterday and staying to help with AJ. They're nice, but they can be…"

"A bit much?"

"Yeah. Way too much. For me, anyway." He wiped his hands down his jeans. "Hey, what are you doing later?"

"Nothing." Anticipation thrummed in her veins. Did he miss her, too?

"I need to order some furniture. Don't have a clue what would work in my living room."

He wanted her help. She found it satisfying—to be needed. Wanted. Even if it was just to help pick out furniture.

"I can come over if you'd like." She tried not to sound too eager. "We can measure the space and figure out what you need."

"Yeah, that would be great." His gaze took her in, and a delicious shiver slid over her skin. "Should I pick up some dinner first?"

"Why don't you let me get the food? You do what you have to do here, and I'll meet you at the house."

"Sounds great. You can leave Ned with me."

"You got it." She turned to leave, then hesitated. "Are you hungry for anything in particular?"

"Anything. I'm starving."

She chuckled. "I'll take care of it."

Picking up dinner, looking at furniture…it all felt so domestic. And she'd be lying if she said she wasn't anticipating spending time with Randy. But what would happen after he moved in?

He wouldn't need her anymore. And she'd be left on her own.

Blue sky, dog at his side, great day back at the store. And now Hannah was helping him pick out furniture. Yeah, he couldn't ask for more.

The breeze cooled Randy's face as he drove with the windows down to the house. The doctor's office had called earlier to let him know the doctor had ordered a few tests before his appointment next week, so he'd scheduled them for Wednesday. Now that his part-time employee, Finn, was back, Randy wouldn't have to worry about the store when he drove an hour away to the hospital for the tests.

He hadn't experienced any symptoms for the past two days. He didn't fear keeling over the way he had a week ago.

Maybe he *could* look forward to the future. Ask Hannah out on a real date. Think about having more than just a house and the store.

Think about a wife.

His throat grew tight. Was he deluding himself? The disease still lurked in his body.

But it had been a while since he'd tried medication. There could be better treatments. Drugs that didn't produce the terrible side effects he'd dealt with last time. Something to prolong his life.

"What do you think, Ned? Am I a fool for liking your owner so much?"

Ned's tongue hung out of his mouth, and he licked his doggy lips. Randy would take that as a yes.

"I need a dog like you by my side." The drive came into view, and he turned down it, marveling at the incredible vistas surrounding him.

In another week, he'd be living here.

Hannah's Jeep was already parked, and she pulled a paper bag out of the passenger seat before waving to him.

He stopped his truck next to the Jeep. He and Ned joined her and Barley on the front porch. The puppy had circled around her legs, roping her with his leash. She was about to either burst out laughing or explode. He wasn't sure which.

"Here, let me help." Randy took the bag from her hands.

"Thanks." She smiled, stepping out of the loop the leash had made, and led the puppy to the front lawn. "This might take a minute."

"No problem." He opened the door for Ned and took the food to the kitchen.

The countertops had been installed! He circled around to take it all in, amazed at how close the house was to being finished.

"He actually went to the bathroom for me." Hannah came into the kitchen with Barley by her side. When she reached the island, she stopped. "Wow."

"My first time seeing it, too." He set out napkins next to the food containers. "Floors are getting started tomorrow."

"Do you have a move-in date?"

"I told the guys to save next Monday night for me. If all goes well, I'll be living here in one week."

"One week." She circled the island, trailing a finger across it, and stepped over to the cabinets. She opened them one by one, then turned to him with a radiant smile. "This is an absolute dream, Randy. I love it."

An intense feeling he couldn't identify swamped him. Looking at her, all bright and happy and sunny and pure Hannah, drove every thought out of his head but one.

She belonged in this house.

And he couldn't think of a single reason why she shouldn't be here.

Long-term.

He closed the distance between them, softly touched her cheek and gazed into those sparkling blue eyes.

Excitement and nervousness warred in them, and he dropped his hand to caress her arm while his other hand slipped around her waist. His face was inches from her.

"I like you." His voice was low, raspy. He half expected her to toss out something sarcastic, but she moistened her lips and blinked up at him.

"I like you, too."

And the only thing he could think to do was to kiss her. Lowering his mouth to hers, he sensed her quick intake of breath, and he pressed her closer to him. The kiss was slow and sweet and right. Her hands crept up to his shoulders as she kissed him back. The sensations flooding him told him this was what he'd been waiting for. This woman. This kiss.

He tasted a hint of lemonade on her lips. He wanted to laugh at how right, how simple it was with her.

When she broke away, he realized how breathless he felt.

"Um, I think we have an audience." Hannah pointed to his left, where Ned and Barley sat looking up at them.

He burst into laughter. Hannah did, too.

For the next couple of hours, they ate enchiladas, measured the living room and sat in chairs in the backyard, scrolling through Randy's phone, looking for furniture.

"A sectional would work great in there." Hannah kept an eye on both dogs, who were nosing around the grass. Whenever Barley began to stray, Ned herded him back.

"Will it fit?"

"What about that one?" She leaned over his arm and pointed to a gray sectional on the screen. "It would seat a lot of people. And you could buy an armchair for the corner."

"I wish I could try it out. I don't like a stiff couch. And I'm going to miss the recliner."

"If you want to make the drive to test them…"

"No." He didn't have time to drive to a bigger city to try out furniture.

"Look! They have a matching recliner." She pointed again. "See?"

"Doesn't look like a recliner. Looks like a regular chair to me."

"It isn't. Swipe through the other pictures."

He realized she was right. It was a recliner.

"Sold." He put his phone away and turned to her. The time seemed ripe to bring up something else on his mind. He'd been wanting to do this for a while. "Do you have a date for Sawyer's wedding?"

"What?" An adorable crinkle formed above the bridge of her nose.

He shifted to face her. "Do. You. Have. A. Date. For. Sawyer's. Wedding?"

Wide-eyed, she shook her head.

"Want to be mine?"

She nodded.

"Well, this is a first. Hannah Carr speechless." His lips curved into a grin. "Rehearsal dinner, too? I'll pick you up for both."

"Is this a date?" Her forehead scrunched in confusion.

Didn't she want to be his date? He'd gotten the impression she'd enjoyed his kiss earlier. Maybe he shouldn't have assumed he was special to her.

"Yeah, it's a date, unless you don't want it to be."

"Don't put words in my mouth, Randy Watkins."

"There's enough words in there—no need for me to put more in." He reached over and entwined his fingers with hers.

"Yes, I'll be your date." A shyness seemed to overcome her, and it surprised him. Whatever he knew about Hannah, shyness wasn't part of it.

Or was she having second thoughts? Had he read her wrong?

"This house…" She was fighting for the words. "The dogs love running around out here. It's a good yard for kids."

Kids?

They'd shared a kiss, and she was talking about kids?

"Don't you mean dogs?" He kept his tone breezy, but her words rocketed his anxiety into gear.

"Those, too." She was looking ahead, and her profile had a wistfulness he hadn't seen before.

Ned loped toward them, and Barley followed, thinking it was a game. Ned bypassed Hannah and sat next to Randy.

Kids and dogs. All because of a date for the wedding. What had he been thinking?

He had a heart condition. One he hadn't told anyone about. And he had no business pretending to be an ordinary guy.

A relationship with Hannah would mean honesty. Coming clean about his health.

But would that be fair to her? Making her worry needlessly about something she couldn't control?

Finding his father lifeless, his body cold, his eyes staring ahead at nothing, had changed Randy in ways he'd never be able to verbalize. He couldn't stand the thought of putting Hannah or any of his loved ones through that.

"Is something wrong?" she asked.

"No."

"You got tense when I mentioned kids."

"No, I didn't. You're reading into things. Thinking too much," he said, standing abruptly. "Let's just enjoy the moment."

Ned licked his hand, and shame overcame him.

He'd told himself he wouldn't be selfish. Wouldn't toy with her emotions. Yet, that was what he was doing.

Could he have forever or not?

He didn't know. He just didn't know.

"Randy's going to be my date for the wedding." Hannah watched the reactions of the other ladies around the table in the showroom of Mayer Canyon Candles the next night. The candle business was in a pole barn on the Mayer family ranch. Reagan and Holly Mayer had set up a large table in the showroom to make decorations for Tess's reception. Tess and Hannah's sister-in-law Leann were also there to help.

Tess dropped the netting she held. Reagan got a dreamy expression on her face. Holly let out a small squeal.

"That's wonderful," Leann raved. "You two are perfect for each other."

"Hold up." She loved their enthusiasm, but it might be misplaced. "It's a date. A plus-one thing. That's it."

After she came home last night, she'd replayed his kiss over and over in her mind. It had been such an amazing kiss. A romantic one. Randy had been tender and giving and his arms had felt so strong, and he'd smelled incredible, and all she could do was picture herself with him in his beautiful house forever.

She'd mentally moved in last night.

But then she'd spoiled it by mentioning kids. And he'd said the words she never wanted to hear again. *You're thinking too much.*

Yeah, she was a thinker, a planner, a doer.

It was the *too much* that had given her pause.

Did every guy consider her too much?

Was she too much?

"Tell us everything," Reagan said.

Hannah zoomed back to the present and realized all of the ladies had scooted their chairs closer and were watching her expectantly. She lunged for another roll of wired tape to shape into a bow. "There's nothing to tell."

The way they were staring at her felt like an interrogation. This was getting weird.

"Did he ask you to be his date?" Tess asked. "Or was it casual, like, hey, we should go together to the wedding?"

"No, he asked me." At least she had that going for her. A murmur of approval rippled through the group.

"Have you been on a date, yet?" Reagan looked positively ecstatic.

"Uh, no." She didn't think anything they'd done constituted a date.

"Taking care of the baby and building the house must have gotten his mind moving in the right direction." Holly had such an easy way about her. "Do you like him?"

"Yeah. Sure." Of course! She liked him too much. *Too much.* Always too much.

"Well, don't get so excited there." Leann rolled her eyes. "Does your mom know?"

"I called her last night."

"I'm shocked she didn't tell me."

"I asked her not to. I don't want it to become this big deal. Really, it isn't. He's picking me up for the rehearsal and the wedding, that's it."

"So, it's two dates." Reagan sounded triumphant.

"I guess." She lifted her right shoulder in a shrug. She wanted to enjoy this and get wrapped up in their enthusiasm, but she couldn't. Her heart was too easily misled. This—this reading into every detail of a guy's intentions— had led to pain before.

"Yeah, but you've been spending a lot of time together." Leann reached over and selected a glass votive holder. "Helping him at the store, helping him paint, helping with the baby. Hmm…did I miss something? Have you had the hots for him all along?"

"No!" Her cheeks were surely on fire. "Austin had an emergency, and I had free time. And any one of you would have babysat that darling baby if you had the summer free like I do."

"Can't argue with you about that. I saw AJ in church and had to stop myself from begging to hold the little guy." Tess got a faraway look in her eyes. "I hope Sawyer wants kids soon."

Kids. The word landed in Hannah's stomach like a concrete slab.

Did Randy have something against kids? She'd seen him with AJ, so loving and gentle and patient. He adored the baby.

She'd just rushed into a conversation he wasn't ready for, that was all.

Tess pointed to her. "Well, you wait, when word gets around town you're dating—"

"We're not dating."

"Has he kissed you?" Reagan asked, arranging netting the way Tess had shown them and setting a votive holder in the center.

Hannah was *not* answering that.

"He has, hasn't he?" Holly's eyes grew round. "Oh, Hannah, he likes you."

The words danced around her heart, but she didn't dare get her hopes up.

"Well, why wouldn't he like her?" Leann waved away the idea as ludicrous. "If he's smart, he'll snatch her up right quick."

"You make me sound like a kidnapping victim." Hannah shook her head.

"Leann's just saying you're a prize, and we all know it." Holly wrapped ribbon around a vase. "You deserve a man who knows it, too."

Her mom had always told her there was someone for everyone. In recent years, she'd doubted it.

"There's someone for everyone," Reagan said. Had she read her mind? "At least, that's what Mom tells me."

"Your mom and mine must be sisters separated at birth." Hannah resumed shaping the ribbon into a bow. "Mine says it all the time."

"What if they're wrong?" Reagan bit her lower lip.

"Then we'll have our own fun."

"Something tells me the local single women will be dwindling from here on out." Tess wore an innocent expression. "You, missy—" Tess pointed to Hannah "—are not escaping, either. Randy's your man. Which leaves… Reagan. Who can we pair you up with?"

"Mac!" Leann grinned.

"No." Reagan's head shook rapidly. "He's Jet's age. Way too old for me."

"Yeah, Mac's a real grandpa." Tess rolled her eyes. "He's not *that* old."

They tossed names around until all of them were laughing hysterically.

Hannah loved them all, but what if they were wrong? No matter how much she liked the idea of Randy being her man, she wasn't sure of him. And she didn't know why.

## Chapter Nine

If he could make it through this move without having a heart attack, Randy would drop to his knees and kiss the ground, anthills and all. Why had he thought moving into the new house the night before his first doctor's appointment in five years was wise?

"Where do you want this?" Jet held one end of a dresser and Blaine the other.

"Master bedroom. Just set it next to the window." As soon as they got it in the house, he went back to the driveway and pressed two fingers to check the pulse in his neck. Beating way too fast.

It had been a whirlwind of a week. He'd picked up Ned each morning, and Hannah stopped by at lunchtime to take him home. Whenever Randy finished up at the store, he'd head to the ranch to play with the baby before either packing his stuff or finishing up odds and ends at the house. Last week he'd put a rush order on the appliances, and they'd been installed this morning. On Saturday, the guys had hosted a bachelor party for Sawyer at Mac's place. It had been a good time.

But through it all, he hadn't been able to get two things off his mind.

Hannah. And the medical tests he'd had done on Wednesday.

He'd find out the results tomorrow. The doctor was going over them with him at the appointment. The mere thought of what he might find out gripped his chest.

Where was Ned when he needed him?

Hannah hadn't arrived, yet. They hadn't seen much of each other all week, other than when they exchanged Ned. He missed her. Hoped after this move he'd get to spend more time with her. If the doctor's visit went well…

A lick on his hand surprised him in the best possible way. "Ned!"

"Sometimes I think you like my dog more than me." Hannah smiled playfully.

"Never." He drew close and kissed her cheek. "Thanks for coming."

"Wouldn't miss it." She flushed in the prettiest way.

"Where's Barley?"

"With my parents. He's come a long way since I got him, but he still has a long way to go. The online meeting with the other puppy raisers yesterday made me feel better about his progress. Everyone else is dealing with potty-training issues, too. Well, except for Liz, who apparently is perfect."

"I'm glad."

They made their way to his truck, where Austin and Mac were sliding boxes toward the lowered tailgate.

"Oh, hi, Hannah," Austin said, wincing as he stepped down.

"Hey, what did we talk about?" Randy fake-punched Austin's arm. "Don't hurt your ankle."

"It's fine. Completely healed." His slight limp said otherwise.

"Yeah, well, I'm not getting up in the night with AJ if you sprain it again."

"It's not AJ you're worried about. You just don't want to check cattle all day."

"Believe it or not, the cows grew on me." Randy hefted one of the boxes in his arms and carried it toward the porch. He glanced at Hannah. "Reagan and Holly are in the kitchen if you want to join them."

"I will." Her eager expression almost made him drop the box, and he tracked her graceful movements as she continued up the steps and through the open door.

Where was he going with this box again? He checked. Master bedroom. Right.

He carried it upstairs, then jogged back down, pausing in the hall as feminine voices mingled.

"This kitchen is gorgeous." He recognized Reagan's soft-spoken voice. "Makes me want to fill it up with gadgets."

"Speaking of gadgets," Holly said. "I hope Randy has more kitchen stuff than this. Where are his pans? Where are the mixing bowls? I've unpacked four glasses, six mugs, three plates and a set of salt and pepper shakers. I don't see anything else for the kitchen."

"Maybe there's more in one of the trucks." Reagan's voice grew muffled. "Nothing a good grocery run won't fix."

He went back outside. He supposed they were right. His entire life he'd lived in a fully stocked house. He didn't have much to call his own. What kind of equipment would he need to cook?

A grill. A new set of tongs. Spatula. Probably a big platter for steaks and burgers.

He drew his eyebrows together as the list grew. A coffeemaker, a skillet, toaster, hot pads...

On the sidewalk, he picked up his pace, trying to remember everything so he could write it down later. Out of the blue, Ned appeared at his side, and he took a deep breath, but his adrenaline continued to climb.

"Grab an end of this, will you?" Blaine stood in the back of the bed of Jet's truck. Randy gripped the end of the box spring, and they maneuvered it to the edge. Blaine hopped down onto the pavement and lifted his end out of the truck. Randy followed.

"Don't think we didn't see that back there." Blaine smirked.

"What?"

"Kissing Hannah's cheek. Reagan told me she's your date for the wedding."

"Yeah, what about it?" Randy walked backward, glancing over his shoulder often, easily carrying his end of the box spring.

"Nothing. I was surprised. That's all. What happened to *I'm never getting married*?" Blaine's voice lilted at the end.

Good question. What *had* happened to it?

"Can we just move my stuff in?" He wasn't having this conversation with so many people around.

"Fine. First Sawyer proposes to Tess. Then Jet starts dating Holly. Now you're into Hannah. I don't think I can trust any of you guys when it comes to women."

Near the door, Austin held a plastic bin. "What's this about not trusting us?"

"Never mind," Randy said. As soon as he cleared the front doorway, he shifted toward the staircase.

"To the left," Blaine yelled. "I don't want to hit the door."

He tried to angle the box spring and almost dropped it. *Stupid, bulky bed...* Grunting, he gripped it tighter. Slowly, they got it up the stairs and into the bedroom where Jet finished putting the bed frame together.

"Think I got it." Jet rose off the floor, then pressed his hands on it to check for sturdiness. "It's not going anywhere. Go ahead and put the box spring on it."

After they centered it on the frame, Jet and Blaine left the room.

Randy stayed where he was. His heartbeat pounded, and dizziness came over him. Ned walked into the room and licked his hand, then nudged it repeatedly until Randy lowered himself to the floor where Ned rested his head on Randy's thigh.

When the dizzy sensation passed, he petted the dog absentmindedly until Ned ambled to the door. Hannah stood nearby watching them.

"Hey, there, buddy." She massaged his ears. "I was wondering where you went."

Had Hannah seen him get on the floor? Did she have any idea how woozy he'd felt?

He scrambled to his feet, hoping it wouldn't set off another wave of dizziness. It didn't.

"Are you feeling okay?" she asked.

"Sure. Why?" He turned his attention to the box spring, adjusting it slightly. Even if he wanted to discuss his health with her—which he didn't—this wasn't the time or the place to do it. It depended on what the tests revealed and what the doctor recommended tomorrow. If the news was good, he'd consider talking to her about it.

"The way Ned was sitting—it's an alert." She took a few steps into the room, watching him carefully. "It's something he was trained to do to help his previous owner."

"Yeah?" He tried to keep his tone light. He'd figured that out a while ago. Hannah was too observant for his taste. "I guess old habits die hard, huh?"

"Or maybe Ned knows something you aren't aware of." Worry and tenderness gleamed in her eyes.

"Well, if he senses something, it's probably the stress of trying to get everything moved in." He gestured for her to go back down the hall, and when she did, he followed her to the staircase.

Heading down to the first floor, she paused to look back at him. "Don't overdo it, okay? Ned isn't merely a pet. He's a highly trained dog. He knows when something isn't right."

"I'm fine."

Through narrowed eyes, she stared a moment. Then she continued down the steps. "Are you sleeping here tonight?"

"Yeah, why?"

"I want Ned to stay with you."

He wanted Ned to stay with him, too, but he didn't want Hannah to know why. They reached the bottom and scooted out of the way as Blaine and Jet carried the mattress inside.

"I'm serious, Randy. It will make me feel better." The way she was nibbling her lower lip brought a twinge of guilt at misleading her.

He patted her shoulder. "Relax. You worry too much. I'm fine."

Something hard and painful crossed her face.

What had he said?

Her eyes were full of hurt. "I don't like to be blown off."

"I'm not blowing you off." He raked his fingers through his hair. "Look, if it means that much to you, I'll be happy to keep Ned tonight."

After holding his gaze for a few moments, she nodded. "I don't worry too much. I just care. It's who I am."

With her head high, she strode to the kitchen.

His careless words had hurt her.

"Where do you want this?" Austin carried a small shelf inside.

"Um, set it in one of the empty bedrooms." He had some smoothing over to do with Hannah. And he wasn't sure how to go about it. In the meantime, he had the rest of the truck to unload.

Maybe he'd have the right words after the appointment tomorrow.

"Barley's a fast learner, Hannah." Molly ended a fifteen-minute training session with the little guy the following morning.

"He's smart," Hannah agreed. "Last weekend, I was convinced I was doing everything wrong. He was such a handful! But I can see now that it was hard taking care of the baby and Barley at the same time. Everything's calmed down now that my days are free."

Hannah hadn't stopped by Paws at Your Service for Molly to work with him, but it had been an added bonus.

She'd actually wanted to talk to Molly about what she'd seen between Ned and Randy.

All the signs were there. Something was wrong with Randy, and Ned was detecting it. But what if Hannah was thinking too much…and incorrect? Molly might have some answers.

"He still has a long way to go," Molly warned. "Don't be afraid to challenge him. I want to see him responding to verbal and nonverbal commands more consistently."

The criticism was valid, but it still hurt to hear it. All month she'd adjusted her life to help her friends. Had she lost sight of what was important to her?

She thought of young Jenna and how Duke had not only improved her mobility at school but also bridged the social gap between her and her peers. Plus, Jenna and the dog had a special bond.

Training Barley was important to Hannah. But so were her friends. Her family. And Randy.

She met Molly's gaze. "I'll make a point to specifically work with him on the commands."

"Good. I'm surprised you didn't bring Ned." Molly handed her the leash, and they strolled over to where six full-grown dogs were working with volunteers. "How's he doing?"

"He's good. Actually, that's why I wanted to talk to you today. You remember Randy? My friend who came with me to pick up Barley?"

"Oh, yeah. I remember him. You two make a cute couple."

They made a cute couple? She could feel her cheeks growing warm. They weren't a couple…or were they?

Yesterday when she'd arrived at his house to help with the move, he'd greeted her with a kiss to the cheek. She'd been around him enough to know he didn't greet any of the other women like that.

But then, their goodbyes last night had been nothing special. He'd thanked everyone for coming to help out, and she'd lingered for a few minutes. But neither spoke, and it grew awkward until he'd asked her if she still wanted to leave Ned with him for the night. When she affirmed it, he told her they'd better get his food. He'd followed her to her apartment, taken the food and toys, looked like he wanted to say something, thought better of it and left with a simple goodbye.

Maybe she should have kept her thoughts about his health to herself. Was she overthinking it? Reading something into his situation that wasn't there?

"Ned's really taken to Randy," Hannah said. "In fact, I've noticed Ned licking his hands several times, usually when Randy gets flustered."

"Sounds like he's alerting." Molly paused near the gate of the training enclosure.

"That's what I thought." At least Molly didn't think she was being dramatic. "I mentioned it to Randy, and he acted like I was an idiot."

"He might not know anything's wrong." Exactly what she feared. "Or Ned could be picking up on general anxiety. He's the one you were helping out at the store, right? Has he had other upheavals to his life lately?"

"Yes, he has. His brother was gone for a week, leaving him to take care of the ranch. Then the baby arrived, and he was trying to finish his house…"

"Yeah, all that would stress out the mellowest person." Molly gave her an understanding smile. "You're worried about him, aren't you?"

She nodded. "Ned's going to the store with him every morning, and I asked him to keep the dog last night."

"How does Ned seem around him?"

"Happy. Honestly, I think he likes Randy more than me." It sounded petty saying it out loud.

She chuckled. "It might seem that way, but the poor dog's probably feeling kind of lost. Helping Randy through a stressful time might be exactly what they both need."

"I hope so." They watched the training session while Barley sniffed the gate. "What if it's more than stress, though?"

"Life will calm down for him. Try not to worry." She patted her arm.

It was true. Life would calm down. Randy no longer had to worry about the ranch or taking care of AJ or finishing projects around the house.

This weekend was the wedding. Friday night was the rehearsal dinner, and Saturday the ceremony and reception. Maybe she'd ask Randy to have Ned stay with him until Friday afternoon. She'd already enlisted her parents to keep the dogs Friday and Saturday since she was in the wedding party and wouldn't have much time for them.

But if he thought she only wanted him to keep the dog this week because she was worried about his health, he might refuse.

She could always tell him she needed more time to train Barley. It would be the truth.

But it wouldn't be the whole truth.

Her conscience jabbed her. *God, I know what You're telling me. There's the right way to do things and the wrong way. Being less than honest with Randy would be wrong. But what if I drive him away?*

If Randy didn't like the fact she was concerned about him, too bad. She wasn't going to tamp down her personality to please him.

She hadn't tamped it down for anyone else, either. And look where it had gotten her.

Unfortunately, she liked Randy a lot.

Too much.

There were the words she loathed again.

Too much.

Why was everything about her too much?

"Five years between echocardiograms is too long." Dr. Bates typed something into his laptop then turned to Randy.

Sitting on the examination table, Randy remained silent. The hair on his arms rose from the smell of rubbing alcohol, the indignity of the paper gown and the dread of whatever the doctor was about to say.

The nurse had taken his vitals—blood pressure was high, no shock there—and the doctor had done the exam. Now Randy was waiting for the verdict.

Dr. Bates held the laptop and clicked through a screen. "Looking at the test results, I can see signs of the ventricle walls thickening compared to your previous tests."

The bottom dropped out of his stomach.

He was getting worse.

He'd known it.

He'd known for years he'd die young.

"...let's try a combination of medications to help reduce how strongly your heart is squeezing and to slow the heart rate so it can pump better..."

"How long do I have?" The words came out harsh.

"What do you mean?" The doctor frowned.

"Five years? Ten?"

"Before you potentially develop symptoms requiring a pacemaker?"

Pacemaker? What? "Before I die."

"Die?" He set the laptop on the counter behind him and spun back to face Randy. "I didn't say anything about dying. Haven't you been listening?"

Had he been listening? He'd heard ventricles thickening and medication and tuned out the rest.

"Your condition is manageable at this point. Try the medications. They've proven effective in preventing fatal heart attacks."

He struggled to take in what the doctor was saying. A cold sweat broke out at his hairline. Medications...what had he said about a pacemaker? "Would a pacemaker prolong my life? Shouldn't we put one in now?"

"No. The symptoms aren't there for me to order one. It wouldn't help you. Now, if over time you develop an arrhythmia, we'll look into it. But there are other things to try first, like a septal myectomy, and that's only if the medications don't help. None of that is necessary right now."

"So what are you saying? My heart is okay?"

He sighed. "The hypertrophic cardiomyopathy has gotten worse, but it's still at a manageable level. I'm prescribing two medications. Together they will greatly improve your chances of not only preventing a heart attack, but surviving one in the event you do have one. I'll call them into the pharmacy, and you can start them today."

Randy chewed on everything the doctor said, but his head still had trouble taking it all in. For years he'd been convinced there was nothing he could do.

"No surgery?"

"No."

"These medications—they'll lessen my chances of a sudden heart attack?"

"Yes."

He remembered the side effects of the last medication he'd been on. He'd only tried it for a few days, and it had been terrible. He'd felt like he was in a fog. To relax, he'd gone fishing and gotten disoriented. Collapsed on the banks of a creek. What if he'd been fly-fishing? He could have drowned.

That night he'd chucked the little orange bottle in the bottom of a drawer and never touched the pills again.

Would this time be different?

"You look concerned," the doctor said. "Any questions I can answer?"

"The meds," he said, "will I be able to think clearly? I don't want to be groggy or anything."

"There will be an adjustment period, but you can expect any side effects to be mild." He then went on to describe the most common problems. "Dry mouth, cold hands and feet, drowsiness, light-headedness, stomach pain, your heartbeat might seem slower. If you experience any of these symptoms, call me. Regardless, I want you to come back next month for a checkup."

Everything the doctor said was becoming clear. Hope sprouted deep inside him.

If the medications worked, all the things he wanted—a relationship with Hannah, marriage, maybe even kids—became possible.

"Okay, let's do it." Randy exhaled loudly.

After talking for a few more minutes, the doctor left the room. Randy got ready as the doctor's words chased around his mind.

Would the medications make a difference? How would he know? Could he trust them?

He supposed he was about to find out.

"I need you to keep an eye on Randy for me, Ned. Can you do that?" The dog was so smart, she half expected him to reply. Hannah drove to Randy's place after supper. He didn't know she was coming, and her nerves snapped, crackled and popped all the way there. The dogs were in the back seat. She glanced in the rearview mirror at them. Shaking her head, she focused on the road.

What could she say to Randy to get him to agree to keep Ned for the next couple of days?

Ever since talking to Molly, she'd grown more certain Ned sensed symptoms in Randy, whether they were stress-related or something more serious. Which led to the next dilemma. Should she mention getting a physical to Randy?

She'd grown up with stubborn men. Her father acted like he was invincible, and on more than one occasion, Mom had laid down the law with Dad about getting a checkup. Having a brother who was a doctor here in town helped. But Hannah didn't have that kind of relationship with Randy, and from their past few interactions, she doubted he'd listen to her.

He'd probably just accuse her of thinking too much or worrying too much.

Maybe he was blowing off reality too much. Did he ever think of that?

*That's not fair and you know it.*

Sighing, she turned down his drive then parked near the house. She let the dogs out of the back seat, took Barley to the front yard to do his business, then headed up to the porch and knocked.

A light breeze teased the ends of her hair. His truck was there, so she figured he was home. She knocked again.

The light thumps of footsteps grew closer, and then the door opened.

"What are you doing here?" His eyes held pleasant surprise as he stepped aside. "Want to come in?"

"If you're not busy." She ignored her hammering heartbeat.

"I'm not busy." He grinned, and a warm glow spread through her core. "You can let the dogs loose if you want."

In a T-shirt, jeans and bare feet, he seemed even more impossibly handsome than she could take. Every other guy paled in comparison.

Ned waited patiently for Randy to pet him, which he did, and Hannah took the opportunity to let Barley off the leash. The pup scampered down the hall to the kitchen. She followed him to make sure he didn't get into trouble.

"What brings you by?" Randy joined her and leaned against the island.

"Thought I'd see how the unpacking is going." She mentally cringed. Why didn't she just come out and tell him the truth?

According to her mother, timing was everything. She'd go with that, not the fact she was nervous.

"It's easy to unpack everything when you don't have much. I've been making a list of things I need to buy." He grabbed a pad of paper and pen off the counter then sat on a stool at the island.

"Like what?" She sat next to him, peering over his arm at the list.

"Towels—I brought one with me from home." He shrugged. "But I have two and a half bathrooms."

She laughed. "Yeah, one won't cut it. What else?"

He read the list and turned to look at her. Her gaze locked on his lips, and memories of his kiss flooded her. Sitting close to him, feeling the warmth of his skin, smelling the faint scent of spice, seeing the interest in his eyes—it made her want to repeat that kiss.

"How's AJ?" she asked, trying to get her mind elsewhere.

"Great. He's sleeping better. Austin says he's only getting up once in the night. Cassie's been amazing. I don't know what we'd do without her. She and AJ bonded instantly."

"I'm glad to hear it. I'll have to text her to see if I can stop by soon." She missed AJ already. And she liked Cassie. Wanted to make her feel welcome now that she was back in town. "I miss the baby."

He tucked her hair behind her ear, the light touch sending a shiver down her spine. "I miss you."

"I miss you, too." Why did she feel so shy all of a sudden? If there was one thing Hannah was not, it was shy.

His lids lowered slightly. "About the other night—I'm sorry."

"I am, too."

"I've had so much going on, I just…"

"Yeah, I know." She figured this would be the best opening she'd get to confront him about Ned and her fears. "I'd feel better if you kept Ned with you until Friday afternoon."

Randy leaned away from her, his face twisting in confusion. "Why?"

It would be so easy to make up an excuse, but it wasn't her way. "I'm worried about you."

His jaw tightened and she could sense the emotional distance growing between them. "I told you not to worry."

"I know you don't want to hear this and you might think I'm reading into things, but I see how Ned is with you. He's so happy when you're together."

Randy's expression softened.

"And I'm convinced it's because you've given him a purpose again. He's spent his entire life warning his owner about medical problems. This might sound strange, but I believe he's picking up on stress signals you might not realize are happening."

She stiffened, waiting for his reaction.

"You're probably right." He sighed, nodding. "It's been a stressful couple of weeks."

Relief spilled through her. "It might not be a bad idea to go to the doctor. In case Ned's picking up on more than just stress."

"Nah." He waved her off. "I'm fine."

Tempted to pinch the bridge of her nose, she tried to think how she could get through to him.

"What if you're not, though?" she asked quietly. "I care about you."

A shadow passed over his face. She wished she knew what he was thinking.

"I'll keep Ned." His tone implied the conversation was over.

She wanted to press the matter, convince him to go to the doctor, but she supposed she should quit while she was ahead.

"I brought his supplies. I told Mom and Dad I'd bring the dogs to the ranch on Friday afternoon. They're watching them for me until Sunday morning, so I can concentrate on the wedding."

"Okay. I'm closing shop early on Friday, so just come through the back whenever you want to get him." He nodded. "What time should I pick you up for the rehearsal?"

"How about five?"

"Done." He pointed to the patio door. "Want to sit out back and watch the sunset? The dogs can play out there."

"Yeah." She couldn't think of anything she'd like more. Besides having Randy agree to make a doctor's appointment. She'd take what she could get. "I'd love that."

Ned would be here watching over him for the next few days. So why did she still have a sinking feeling in her gut?

Maybe she *did* worry too much.

She didn't want to be one of those her-way-or-the-highway people. But she didn't think she could stand by and worry about someone she cared about without trying to convince them to get help.

Randy didn't want help, though.

And there wasn't anything she could say to change it.

# Chapter Ten

He'd been slammed all day. Customers from far away had filled the store, wanting information on the lures he'd showcased in the video he'd posted this week. Fridays tended to be busy, though. A lot of people stopped in to get all their fishing gear for the weekend. Randy normally could handle the nonstop questions and steady sales. Something was off with him, today, though. Something physical. And it worried him.

The sensation of light-headedness seized him again, and he gripped the edge of the counter, forcing himself to focus on the cash register. Ned had been chilling out behind the counter, but the dog came over and sat next to him. A sure sign whatever was going on wasn't all in his head.

"Go ahead and insert your card." Randy gestured to the man on the other side of the counter.

The retired couple from Sheridan bickered about how to insert the chip, with the wife insisting her husband had it in backward. Finally, the man snapped at her. "I know how to use a credit card."

"It's in wrong." She glared at her husband. He glared back.

"The system's been slow today," he said. *Just get through this transaction and you can sit down for a few minutes.* "Do you mind trying again? The chip goes in first."

The man's face was already tomato-red, but he flipped the card around, and a chiming sound meant it went through. Randy bagged their items and thanked them for their business. "Come back anytime."

"We will." The woman beamed, already over the credit-card drama he'd just witnessed.

"How do you feel about this rod?" Joe Schlock approached the counter. He held a fly-fishing rod in his hand. "Good for trout?"

Randy's hands were ice-cold, and his fingers started to shake. Ned licked his hand. He blew out a light breath. "Yes, it's a good one." He doubted Joe would buy a rod today. The man liked to come in and handle them all, but he typically purchased books and lures.

"Say, where did Finn run off to?" Joe looked around.

"He left early. He's in charge tomorrow, so I told him to take the rest of the day off."

"It's too bad Hannah's not working here anymore. She's got a good head on her shoulders."

"Yes, she really helped me out of a jam." She did have a good head on her shoulders. And a pretty face. And a kind heart. And…another wave of light-headedness came over him. Ned licked the back of his hand. "What time is it?"

Joe checked his watch. "Almost four. Hey, weren't you closing early today? I saw the sign out front."

"Yeah. For Sawyer's wedding rehearsal." He felt funny, like he might pass out. *Not now. Get through this. God, don't do this to me.*

"Well, I'd better get moving so you can lock up." Joe walked back and put the rod away. "Have fun at the wedding."

"I will. Thanks." As soon as Joe left, Randy made his way to the front door and locked it, flipping the Closed sign on the door. Then he backtracked to the counter.

Normally, he'd tidy up for a few minutes, unpack the boxes that had arrived earlier and add up the receipts. But all he could do was sit on the stool and stare at the trembling hands in his lap.

Ned had followed him and was sitting right next to the stool, watching him.

When was Hannah supposed to get here?

Soon, he thought.

He didn't want her seeing him like this.

No one else had picked up on his symptoms today, but she would.

Maybe he just needed to clear his head for a minute. Sit there and not do anything. Attempting a deep breath, he tried to concentrate.

Randy was glad Hannah had insisted he keep the dog all week. Every night she'd driven to the house for a few hours, and they'd sat on the back deck with the dogs and talked.

It had felt natural. Right.

They'd laughed about old memories of things that happened around town. They'd shared small things like their favorite colors—hers was lavender, his was dark blue—

and their taste in music and favorite movies. He hadn't been surprised to find out she couldn't get enough of re-runs of television shows like *Law & Order* and *CSI*. She wasn't much of a reader—neither was he—but when she did read, she preferred whodunits.

They'd shared deeper things, too, like what it was like growing up and how their faith shaped them. Over the past six months, he'd grown more vocal about his deep love for Jesus, and she seemed to think it was a good thing.

The light-headedness and trembling sensation weren't as bad now. He had a lot to do before closing the store, and he needed time to get ready for the rehearsal tonight.

As soon as it was over, he planned on telling Hannah two things. One, he had a heart condition that might or might not kill him before he grew old. And two, he loved her.

As soon as he stood, his fingers trembled again, and the woozy feeling slammed him. Ned licked his hand, nudging it. His heartbeat accelerated to the point he feared it might be out of control.

What was happening?

It was beating too fast. He swayed. Reached back to brace himself against the wall, but nothing was there.

Was this it?

His vision blurred. His knees buckled.

And he didn't register Ned's tongue on his hand. He no longer comprehended anything as his body crumpled to the floor.

Tonight was the night! Hannah's pulse raced with anticipation as she parked behind Randy's store to pick up Ned. In a little while, he'd be taking her to Tess and Sawyer's wedding rehearsal. She was thrilled for them.

She was also thrilled to have a date. A real date! With the most gorgeous, incredible guy she'd ever met. Their relaxed conversations on his back deck all week had revealed the truth.

She was halfway in love with him.

Maybe all the way.

And why not? There was nothing to fear. Randy was single, and so was she. They got along great. They had the same values.

Grinning, she stepped into the hot sunshine and opened the door to let Barley out. He trotted on his leash beside her as they closed the distance to the back door. She opened it, calling, "Hello? I'm here."

With confident strides, she made her way down the hall. Where was Randy?

Ned raced to her side and barked, then disappeared behind the counter. Her stomach plummeted, and her heart started pounding. Something was wrong. She dropped Barley's leash, and he, too, ran behind the counter.

The instant she saw Randy's body, she dropped to her knees, cradling his head on her lap. Ned was licking his hand and mouthing it.

"Randy, can you hear me?" Panic flooded her. She'd been trained in CPR, but what was she supposed to do? She couldn't remember a thing. *Think!*

Barley barked and licked Randy's face.

*God, I don't know what to do. Help me! Help him!*

A calmness overtook her, and she bent so her cheek hovered above his mouth and nose. He was breathing. It was shallow, but the breath was there. She pressed her fingers to his neck and felt a faint pulse. *Thank You, Jesus!*

She stroked his hair. "Wake up, Randy. Can you hear me? Wake up."

Tears dripped on her cheeks, and she barely noticed. Ned came over and used his nose to push her purse closer.

"Good boy." She stroked Ned's neck with one hand and retrieved her cell phone out of her purse with the other. "You're such a good boy. You're getting extra treats after this."

Quickly, she called her brother. He was a doctor. He'd know what to do.

"What's going on?" David answered after two rings.

"Randy's unconscious. I don't know what's wrong. I don't know what to do!" She was getting upset and couldn't help it.

"Hang tight. I'll be right over."

"I'm at his store. Behind the counter. The back door's open."

"Be there in five." And he hung up.

Randy's eyelashes fluttered, and he moaned.

"Shh…just stay where you are. You're going to be okay." She continued stroking his hair, and both dogs sat next to each other a few feet away, playfully rubbing necks with each other. The fact Ned wasn't glued to Randy's side was a relief. She had no doubt he'd be right there if Randy was still in danger.

He pressed his elbow to the floor to sit up.

"I told you to stay where you were." She tried to press him back down, but he wasn't having it.

He wiped his palm down his face. "What was I doing on the floor?"

"I don't know. I think you might have passed out."

"What?" He looked and sounded confused.

"I stopped by to pick up Ned." She knelt in front of him. "David's on the way."

"David?"

"My brother. He'll be able to help." She attempted a smile. With so many questions sprinting through her brain, she was doing her best not to fall apart.

"Hey, don't cry." He reached up and brushed her cheek with his thumb.

She was crying? Didn't surprise her. She threw her arms around his neck. "Oh, Randy, I'm so glad you're okay."

"I'm fine." His voice grew stronger. "Just passed out. No need to worry."

No need to worry? She'd found him unconscious on the floor! Of course she was worried.

The sound of the back door opening had her scrambling to her feet. As soon as David appeared, she hugged him tightly and led him to Randy.

"What's going on?" Her brother wore a button-down shirt with dress slacks, and he carried a medical bag.

"I don't know. One minute I was locking up. The next, I was on the floor."

David pulled out a stethoscope from the bag. "Hannah, do you mind giving us some privacy? Maybe take the dogs outside for a few minutes."

Privacy? But…she wanted to know what was wrong. The way her brother stared at her, though, she knew nothing more would be said between them until she left. She nodded, gathered the dogs and went outside.

As soon as her feet hit the pavement out back, she started to shake.

Finding Randy like that…she shivered. He always seemed so solid. So strong. So reliable.

He claimed he'd just passed out. What if this wasn't the first time it had happened?

Was Randy in denial? Could he be sick?

Would he even tell her if he was?

She took the dogs to the Jeep and rooted around in the back where she kept dog supplies, including treats. She then gave Ned and Barley several each.

"My good boys. You two were awesome back there." She crouched down to their level, petting them both. But she couldn't stop the worries, couldn't shake off the feeling that something was seriously wrong with the man she loved.

There wasn't any question about it. The instant she'd seen him on the floor, she'd known she loved him. And she couldn't imagine life without him.

She just prayed he would be okay.


"Walk me through what happened before you passed out." Dr. Carr finished checking Randy's pulse and listening to his heart, then stepped back and leaned against the counter, the stethoscope dangling around his neck. Randy stood, but his legs were still weak, so he sat on the stool.

He stared into David's eyes, and he knew the jig was up. He couldn't—wouldn't—lie to Hannah's brother. And by telling him, Randy would be forced to be truthful with Hannah. Because there was no way he'd tell her brother about his health situation without being up-front about it with her, too.

He loved her too much to be that cruel.

"I have a heart condition." Randy stared down at his hands. "Same one that killed my dad."

David widened his eyes and dipped his chin slightly for him to continue.

"Hypertrophic cardiomyopathy."

"Are you being treated for it?"

He nodded. "Started meds Tuesday night."

"What medications are they?"

Randy told him.

"Do you know the dosage?"

"Not offhand." He pressed his eyes shut briefly then opened them. "Wait, I took notes on my phone. Let me check." His phone was on the counter near the register, so he grabbed it and scrolled through until he found the note. Then he read it out loud.

"That explains a lot." David frowned. "Tell me about your symptoms again."

"Cold hands. Shaky fingers. Light-headed. Dizzy. I felt foggy. Couldn't keep my thoughts straight." Hearing the words out loud made him realize how much he'd been ignoring what was happening.

"For how long?"

"The dizziness? Off and on for weeks. But the others—the cold, shaking hands, the mental fogginess—those are new."

"How new? Since you started the medications?"

He tried to think back. "Yeah. I guess that's right."

David nodded. "Until you can talk to your doctor, cut the doses of both medications in half. My guess is your body is adjusting to them, and you're dealing with natural side effects."

"Do you think I'm going to have a heart attack?" He watched David's face carefully to see if he thought he was being dumb.

"No, I don't." His tone was serious. "You said you didn't have chest pains, heartburn, shortness of breath or pain in your upper body. The signs of a heart attack weren't there. But you did have typical side effects from the medications you're on. And since you recently started them, I'd say they're the problem. I want you to take it easy tonight."

"Can't. Rehearsal dinner."

"You're going to have to miss it. And if you're still feeling symptoms tomorrow, you're going to have to do the bare minimum at the wedding."

"Sawyer's one of my best friends, man."

"That's why he'll understand you have to sit this one out tonight."

"He doesn't know," Randy practically growled. "No one knows. Not even my brother."

David clapped a hand on his shoulder and looked deep in his eyes. "I won't tell anyone. I took an oath."

He nodded, feeling small and confused.

"I'll let myself out. Call me anytime if you're having symptoms." David picked up his medical bag and turned to leave. "I'll tell Hannah it's okay to come back in."

"Thanks. I really appreciate you coming here."

"Don't mention it." And he left.

Randy braced himself for Hannah to return. He'd kept this secret for years and years, and now he couldn't keep it any longer.

He'd tell it to her straight.

No sugarcoating it.

She deserved to know it all—and he wasn't going to spare a single detail. Seeing her so upset at finding him, well, he knew how that felt.

He hadn't wanted her to find out this way. He'd wanted… what?

He'd wanted to be normal. To have a normal life. With a wife. And kids.

But he wasn't normal, and telling Hannah was going to be the hardest thing he'd ever done. He just prayed she'd understand why he'd kept it from her.

# Chapter Eleven

"You can go in there now." David strode to where Hannah leaned against the back of the Jeep.

"Thanks for coming." She gave him a hug, wanting to demand he tell her what was wrong with Randy, knowing he wouldn't.

He hugged her back and let her go. "You did the right thing, calling me."

"You were the first one I thought of." She tightened her hold on Barley's leash as the pup tried to jump on his leg. "Down, Barley. Is Randy okay?"

"Go see for yourself." David hitched his thumb back. "Hey, weren't you taking the dogs to Mom and Dad's tonight?"

"Yes, but I'll have to do it later." She couldn't think about anything but Randy at the moment.

"I'll drop them off for you."

"You will?" For some reason, his thoughtfulness made her want to start crying again. "Thanks. I'm keeping Ned, though. He's good for Randy."

She opened the back of the Jeep and helped load Barley's stuff into David's truck. Then she handed him Barley's leash, bent to say goodbye to the pup and waited until David had him firmly in hand before hurrying with Ned to the back door of the store.

Her mind crawled with worries. What had caused him to pass out? She thought of all the moments over the past month when he'd been out of breath or flushed or checking his pulse. And all the times Ned had made a point to be right next to him, licking his hand or staring at him.

She braced herself for bad news as she made her way down the hallway.

This was the one time she hoped she really was overthinking things.

Randy stood with his back against the wall behind the cash register. As soon as she saw him, she let go of Ned's leash and launched herself into his arms. He held her close, stroking her hair, and she sank into his embrace, letting him comfort her when she should be the one comforting him.

"You scared me." She leaned back to look up into his eyes. "What happened?"

He put both hands around her waist and lifted her to sit on the stool. She opened her mouth to tell him he shouldn't be lifting anything, but she enjoyed the sensation too much and kept her mouth shut.

"I passed out."

"Yeah, I know that."

"Your brother thinks it was because of my medications."

She frowned. Medications? Why was he taking medications? She studied his face—still on the pale side. And serious. Way too serious.

She wasn't going to like whatever he was about to say.

"I have hypertrophic cardiomyopathy." Did she detect relief in his tone? "The same heart condition that killed my dad."

*Heart condition...killed...dad.* The words jumbled around in her mind but she couldn't make sense of them. What was he saying?

"Okay. So you're on medication. You're treating it. You're not going to die. Do what David said and it will take care of everything..." Words spilled out of her mouth, but she really didn't know what she was saying.

Her chest was locked up so tightly, she could barely breathe.

"No, Hannah. That's not how it works." He was being gentle with her. Too gentle. Speaking slowly, softly, with his hands still at her waist. Fear slithered down her spine.

Her senses sharpened as the truth jelled. In that instant, she smelled the earthy tang of the store, felt the breeze kicked around by the overhead fan, heard a car drive by out front, tasted the bitterness of what Randy was telling her.

He had the same disease that had killed his father.

Tears formed again, and, one by one, dropped to her cheeks. "You're not going to die."

His throat worked, but he didn't respond.

"Tell me you aren't going to die." Her voice rose, and she reached up and gripped his shirt in her hands. "No, Randy, no."

He caught her hands in his and kissed her knuckles. "I don't know, Hannah. For years, I've been aware I'm living on borrowed time. And I made peace with it. Opened this store. Decided to build the house. But lately..." He touched her cheek. "I've been wanting more. So I had more tests done, and I'm trying new meds, but Hannah, I don't have any guarantees."

She shook her head back and forth, trying to make the words disappear. "There has to be something you can do."

"I wish I could tell you what you want to hear, but it is what it is. It's not going to get better. I might be able to manage it. I might not. I'm trying."

"But I love you!" She hadn't meant to blurt it out. Hadn't meant to say it at all. And the way his eyes grew round, she figured he hadn't expected it, either. His shaky inhalation made her want to choke back the words, tuck them away where they were safe. But she couldn't.

He leaned forward and looked her in the eyes. "I love you too much to do this to you."

He loved her? Her heartbeat pounded. He loved her!

"I never should have let it get this far to begin with." His chin dipped to his chest. Then he met her gaze. "When I was nineteen, I promised myself I'd never get married or have kids."

"Nineteen? You've known all these years?" She eased back a few inches. For some reason, she thought he'd found out recently. "And you decided to skip marriage and kids? Why? It doesn't make sense." She tilted her chin up, searching his face for the clues she was obviously missing.

His eyes darkened. "One month after I graduated from high school, I walked into my dad's room to borrow a belt. He usually was working on the ranch before I woke up." He paused, pulling himself together. "The covers had been flung back, but he was in bed. His face was pale, yellowish. His eyes were open, but no one was home."

"Oh, Randy. I'm sorry."

"I couldn't believe it. It was such a shock. I took his hand—cold. I threw my arms around him and tried to force him up, but he'd been dead for a few hours. The

EMTs told me he'd likely had the heart attack right after he'd woken up. He was only forty-eight. We'd arm wrestled two days before, and he'd won. He was in great shape. I couldn't comprehend it."

She'd never really thought about how his dad's death had affected him. She supposed she'd known he'd found his father's body, but she hadn't realized what all it had entailed.

"The coroner told Austin and me that Dad had a sudden heart attack due to hypertrophic cardiomyopathy. It's genetic, so we both got tested. Austin doesn't have it. And I do. But I decided to keep it private. Austin doesn't know. No one does—well, except me, my doctor and now your brother."

"And me," she said softly. "But why wouldn't you at least tell Austin? That's not fair to him."

"Fair?" He edged back slightly. "There's nothing fair about putting all that worry on him when there's nothing either of us can do to change it. I can't change it. You know that, right?"

She did *not* know it. In fact, her fingers itched to get her cell phone out of her purse and start researching cures and treatment right this second.

"I didn't want to tell you." He looked away.

"Well, thanks a lot," she said, hating how snippy she sounded. "Makes me feel great you didn't feel you could trust me with it."

He pointed to her then back to himself. "This—what we have—can't go any further."

"Why not?" She was missing something important, and for the life of her, had no idea what it was.

"Because I couldn't live with myself knowing one day

you'll walk in on my dead body like I did my dad's." His face grew hard.

"Shouldn't I get a say in it?"

"It's genetic, Hannah. There's a fifty percent chance it passes to my kids. Can you honestly say you wouldn't worry every day of your life if you knew one or more of our children have this? No, I won't let that happen."

"But…"

"I won't do it." He backed up, crossing his arms over his chest. "And when you have time to think it through, you'll see I'm right."

He was doing the right thing. The noble thing. If he didn't stand firm now, he'd put her through ten times more pain later. Randy watched her expression harden and girded himself for her response.

She couldn't understand the horror of finding a loved one dead, their body cold, lifeless.

And he'd make sure she'd never understand it.

"Why do you get to make all the rules?" She jabbed her finger at him. "I don't even know how to argue with you. I'm just learning about all this, but it seems you made your decision about me a long time ago."

He had, but after being around her, he'd changed his mind. Well, he'd started to change it. Having her find him unconscious had been the wake-up call he'd needed.

He'd been living in a dream, and he'd woken up.

All of a sudden, he felt tired. Drained. His hands started to tremble.

Ned came over and sat next to him, watching him.

Hannah glanced at Ned then back at Randy. She blinked, then stared at him through hurt eyes. "You acted like I was delusional the other night when I told you I thought Ned was alerting you. You told me I worry too much."

Her tone accused, and he squirmed, reaching back to steady himself against the wall.

"Why didn't you tell me, then?" Her big blue eyes filled with hurt all the way to the brim. All because of him.

"In a house full of our friends? My brother doesn't even know."

"Why is that? He's your best friend. You couldn't tell your best friend?" The way she was staring at him, like he'd kicked a bunny or something, raised his hackles.

"I was protecting him." He shifted his jaw.

"Like you were protecting me?" Disappointment dripped off her. "Like you're still protecting me?"

"Yes," he growled.

"I'm not going to just walk away and act like nothing ever happened between us. I care about you too much."

He clenched his jaw. He never should have let it get this far. Her phone chimed, and she glanced at it.

"Look," Hannah said. "I have to get ready." All the fight went out of her. He hated to see her this way. Hated that he was the one to cause it.

"I'm sorry," he said. "I can't take you to the rehearsal. I told your brother I'd stay home tonight. He thinks the dosage of my medication might be too high for my body to handle, and that's why I passed out."

"I'll drive you home, then," she said, the words clipped. "I don't think it's safe for you to be behind the wheel."

"That's okay." He could sense it all ending—the hope, the taste of the life he'd so wanted.

"No, I'll take you. You're not driving."

"I know, Hannah." The anger rising up wasn't at her.

It was at himself. "I wouldn't put anyone in danger by driving right now. I can get a ride from someone in two seconds flat."

She hiked her purse over her shoulder and gave him a cold glare. "Ned stays with you. If he starts alerting you, call David. I'd tell you to call me, but it's obvious you won't. You're determined to push me away."

A flare of anger sparked. "That's not fair."

"It's not fair what you're doing to me, either."

"C'mon, Hannah. I don't want you spending the rest of your life worrying. Wondering if I'm going to die. Can you imagine if we decided to get married and then had kids? Let's say one of them inherited this disease. It would break you."

"How do you know what would break me?" She stood there still and furious and so beautiful it took his breath away. "I'm not made out of glass."

"You know what I mean." He wanted to take her in his arms, but he didn't. Couldn't. "You deserve better than that."

"All I hear is that you won't consider a future with me because I'll worry, and me worrying about you and our children would be just too much for you to handle." She plunged her hand into her purse and fished out her keys.

"I didn't say that." He reached for her as she pivoted to leave, but she shook his hand away.

"Go home," she said flatly. "Get some rest. I'm not going to ruin this night for Tess and Sawyer. I'll see you tomorrow."

"Hannah, wait."

She looked back over her shoulder at him. "I don't think you're doing this for me at all, Randy. I think it's easier for you. You can use your condition to lock your heart into a box. Life's less complicated if you're alone. You don't have to deal with my feelings inconveniencing you. But you're forgetting something. I'm going to worry about you no matter what because I already love you. That doesn't go away just because you say so."

He had no reply.

"By the way, this isn't over," she said. "We'll talk about it when we both have time to think." And she walked away.

At the sound of the door slamming, he almost sank to his knees.

Mission accomplished. He'd told her about his health, and he'd messed it up in every possible way.

His veins felt jittery, and the light-headed sensation came back. Hannah was right about one thing—he wasn't driving home. It was too late to call Austin or any of the guys. They were all on their way to the rehearsal. First things first. He'd better call Sawyer and let him know he wouldn't be there tonight.

He found his phone and made the call. Kept it brief, assured him he'd be fine and at the wedding tomorrow before hanging up.

Randy's gaze went to the front window. Joe Schlock's truck was parked across the street. He'd probably gone to the Barking Squirrel for a cup of coffee. Maybe he'd be willing to take him home.

Right on cue, Joe exited the diner's door, and Randy strode to the front of the store, unlocked the door and went outside, waving. "Joe."

The man looked up and grinned. "What's going on?"

"Could you give me a lift?"

"Sure." He checked for traffic and crossed the road, stopping in front of Randy. "What's going on?"

He debated how much to tell him and realized he didn't care if Joe knew he'd passed out.

"I had a dizzy spell, and Dr. Carr wants me to take it easy tonight. Mind taking me home?"

"Of course not. You finish whatever you need to do, and I'll bring the truck around the back."

"Thanks." He was surprised Joe hadn't asked what was wrong with him.

He locked up, turned off the lights and, with Ned by his side, made his way to the back of the store where Hannah's perfume lingered. His heart stung. He hated that he'd hurt her. After locking the back door, he took Ned to the back parking lot.

"Hop in." Joe's truck stopped next to him, and Randy and Ned got in. "Sorry to hear you're feeling under the weather."

"Thanks."

He drove ahead and turned onto the road. "It's handy having a gal with a doctor for a brother."

*She's not my gal.*

"Linda's brother was a logger up in Montana. Not as handy."

"Linda was your wife, right?" Randy didn't know much about Joe's past although he'd lived here his entire life.

"Sure was. She ruled the roost, too." He grinned at Randy. "There was no changing her mind when she thought she was right about something."

"You don't sound like you minded."

"She was always right. I miss her." Joe pointed up ahead. "Owl Creek?"

"Yes."

"Never knew how blessed I was until she died. Life

got quiet. No more lemon-drizzle bundt cakes. No more pestering me about changing out of my work pants before sitting on the furniture. No more quiet evenings together, her with her book and me with the newspaper. Didn't have to say a thing. We were comfortable with each other."

"I'm sorry, Joe. How long has she been gone?"

"Twelve years." He grew somber. "I'd give about anything for another day of her ordering me around, baking those cakes, sitting with me in the evenings. I'd even take one of her lectures or one of our fights."

"How did she die?"

"Cancer. We were blessed, though. She went into remission twice before it finally took her."

"Twice?" Randy frowned.

"Yes. She was first diagnosed at forty-seven. Chemo gave her ten years in remission. Then she found a lump under her armpit. Radiation, surgery and more chemo got her through it again. By the time they found it the third time, I think her body was just plumb wore out. I had two more years with her after that, though. Wouldn't trade them for anything."

"This is it." Randy gestured to the drive up ahead. All those years of living under the cloud of cancer. That would be tough.

"Nice property you've got." The truck rumbled down the drive to the house before halting. "If you need me to take you back into town to get your truck, just holler. You have my number."

"Thanks, I will. I appreciate it. I'm sorry about your wife, Joe." He got out, helped Ned down and waved as Joe backed up. The truck disappeared in the distance, and Randy stayed rooted in place.

He felt unmoored, like a boat that had been docked for years and was now drifting at sea.

His house was finished. All the months of planning and watching and working were done.

But living there alone wasn't satisfying. All he could see was Hannah laughing on the porch or helping him measure the living room. Dipping her brush into the paint, cutting in the ceiling, yelling at Barley to not eat a paper towel, sitting on the back deck with him chatting about life.

He'd gotten used to her companionship and, like Joe with Linda, didn't want it to end.

Sighing, he headed up the porch steps and let Ned inside.

Now that Hannah knew about his heart problem, he'd better tell Austin. Randy doubted he could feel worse than he currently did, but life had a funny way of kicking him when he was down. He texted Austin, asking him to stop by after the rehearsal.

And then he went upstairs, sprawled out on his bed and promptly fell asleep.

Surrounded by happy couples, Hannah pushed a bite of cheesecake around her plate in Mac's spotless pole barn. The rehearsal dinner was almost over, thankfully, and she vaguely noted what a charming venue it was. The renovated pole barn obviously wasn't used for anything besides entertaining a crowd.

She shoved the plate away. The dinner had been catered, and the meal would have been delicious if she wasn't full of so much turmoil.

Two hours ago when she'd stood at the front of the church while Tess and Sawyer rehearsed their vows, she'd been thrilled for them even as her spirits slid to a low point. They were in love, and it was obvious Jet and Holly were, too. Hannah would have to be blind not to notice all the flirty smiles they'd exchanged.

It only brought home the fact Randy wasn't there, and even if he had been, they wouldn't be sharing charged glances or smiles the way the other couples had.

He had a heart condition. It wouldn't go away. It could kill him. Maybe years from now. Maybe tomorrow. She had no way of knowing.

The facts had sunk in as the hours had worn on.

She finally understood why he was pushing her away.

"Is everything okay?" Reagan set a plate filled with desserts on the table, pulled out the chair across from her and sat. "You've been really quiet all night."

"Yeah, I'm fine." What a lie. She wasn't fine. And normally she would relish the chance to hash out exactly what the problem was with Reagan, but the words shriveled in her throat.

"What's going on with Randy? I thought he was bringing you tonight." Reagan took a bite of chocolate cake. "Mmm, this is good."

"He's not feeling well and had to stay home." Her voice sounded normal at least.

"Will he be at the wedding?"

"I think so." She hoped so. What if he'd gone home and gotten worse? Or tried to drive and passed out again?

He could be in a ditch.

What if he made it home and collapsed, but this time there was no one to find him?

As panic rose, she forced herself to take a deep breath.

Ned would be there. Ned would get him back on his feet.

Unless Randy couldn't get back on his feet.

Her chest grew uncomfortably tight. Maybe she should call him. Check on him. At the very least, text him.

"Hannah?" Reagan's forehead was lined with concern.

"Sorry." She shook her head, trying to smile. "Just have a lot on my mind. What were you saying?"

Austin chose that moment to stop by their table. "I wanted to thank you again, Hannah, for all the help with AJ."

"I was happy to do it. And Cassie is a pro with him."

"She is. She took a big load off my mind by watching him. We worked out a good schedule now that Bo's back. He's doing all the early chores so I can take care of AJ until she arrives in the morning."

"I'm glad."

"Me, too." He smiled. "I'm going to take off. I've got to stop by Randy's before I head home. Thanks for hooking me up with the babysitter tonight, too."

"You're welcome." Relief hit her that he was going over to Randy's. But selfishly, she wanted to be the one to check on him. She didn't trust herself yet, though.

As much as she wanted to think of herself as brave and competent and caring, all night she'd been wondering if Randy was correct in pumping the brakes on their relationship.

Being with him would mean accepting the fact he could die at any time. And it would also mean possibly not having kids. He didn't seem to want them, wasn't willing to take the chance he'd pass his condition on to them.

The shock of finding him earlier wasn't helping her get clarity, either. His pale face, faint pulse, the way his body was crumpled—she couldn't get it out of her head. And Ned, poor, dear Ned, licking his hand, nudging his arm…

"It's wedding-a-rama around here." Reagan stared off to the side. Hannah forced herself to pay attention. "First my sister, now Tess. I wouldn't be surprised if Holly and my brother aren't far behind."

"I wouldn't be, either. They make a cute couple." Good, a distraction from her thoughts. "Would it be weird for you? I mean, knowing Holly was married to Cody first?" Cody was Reagan's youngest brother, who'd died over a year ago. The family hadn't known Cody had been married to Holly until February, when she and their baby had moved to Mayer Canyon Ranch. Six-month-old Clara was a chubby-cheeked darling.

Hannah wanted a daughter just like her. Four kids would be great. Two boys. Two girls. Or any combination really.

She'd always seen herself with children.

Reagan wore a wistful expression. "I love Holly. Working with her has been such a blessing to us and to the candle business. If Jet married her, it would be the icing on the cake."

Jealousy pinched her as she thought of all her friends whose lives were falling into place. For the past few weeks, she'd thought hers was, too.

"You know, I always thought I'd have the fairy tale." Reagan finished the last bite of her cake. "Lately, I don't see it happening."

A pang of shame hit her. Reagan's dreams hadn't come true, either.

"I know what you mean," Hannah said. "I used to scoff at Mom's *there's someone for everyone* comments, but secretly, I believed it. Now?" She shrugged as guilt hit her. The words felt disloyal to Randy, even though he'd all but broken it off with her.

"What? I thought you and Randy…?" Reagan's eyebrows formed a V.

"We're friends."

"Just friends?"

She nodded, but it wasn't true. She'd never be just friends with Randy.

She loved him too much to go back to being pals. But she didn't know if she could handle a future that might include finding him on the floor. What if Ned couldn't rouse him? Randy's description of finding his father came back. Cold hands, waxy complexion, no pulse…

Fear gripped her veins.

*Stop it!*

"I think I'm going to take off." Hannah inched her chair back and stood. "I'll see you tomorrow."

"You all right?" Reagan gave her a questioning look. She nodded. "Okay. See you tomorrow."

Maybe she *was* made of glass. She loved Randy, but she didn't know if she was strong enough to be the woman he needed. Was she up for a lifetime of worry?

She didn't know.

And if she didn't know, then did she really love him?

Everything she thought to be true about herself had a big question mark next to it. And until she knew for sure, she'd leave Randy alone.

# Chapter Twelve

"What's wrong? Do you have the flu or something?"

Randy sat at the island facing Austin later that night. At his request, Austin had stopped by after the rehearsal dinner. On the way into the kitchen, his brother had caught him up on what to expect at the wedding tomorrow, then proceeded to share the joy of seeing AJ smile for the first time.

"No." Randy looked down at his hands. He'd thought about telling Austin about his heart so many times in the past, but he'd always convinced himself it was better to keep it to himself.

This was going to be a rough conversation.

Would Austin get mad? Storm out of there?

Or would he pity him? Start treating him differently? What if he went into worry mode? Started fussing constantly? Tried to put limits on his life?

Maybe that was what Randy really feared. No longer being treated the same.

"I passed out at the store." He figured it was as good a lead-in as any.

Austin blinked away his shock. "Why?"

"I have the same heart condition Dad did."

"What?" He stood so quickly his stool almost tipped over. "When did you find out? How do you know? What are you doing about it?"

"I found out the summer after Dad died." Randy let it sink in a moment. "I didn't want anyone to know."

"No. No way you kept this from me." Was steam coming out of his ears? Austin ground his teeth together. "So you're telling me you've known you might die for over ten years and you never bothered to tell me? Why would you do that?"

"Because I didn't want you to worry. It was bad enough Dad died unexpectedly. If you thought I might die, too…" He was surprised his voice was this calm. "You'd already been through enough."

"Oh, and I suppose it would be better for me to just walk in on your dead body and have to piece it all together. Are you hearing yourself?" Angry didn't begin to describe him.

"What's worse?" Randy said. "Living with anxiety about my condition and finding me dead, or enjoying life and finding me dead? Both scenarios end the same, Austin. I know you. You'd be thinking about my health constantly."

He paced back and forth near the cabinets. "Not telling me was selfish. I should have known. You should have told me."

"Like I should have known you were practically on a suicide mission in Texas?" Randy's voice rose. "That you're raising someone else's baby as your own?" The hypocrite.

"That's different."

"It's not."

They glared at each other until Austin perched on the stool once more. "Now what? Is it getting worse? Is that why you fainted?"

"No." He didn't want to spill all of it, but he might as well. He owed him the truth. "I decided to try medication again."

"Again?" His voice went up an octave. "Why haven't you been on it this entire time?"

"I tried one five years ago, but it made me sick—really sick—so I quit."

"Well, that was stupid."

"Not from my point of view," Randy said. "I had tests done last week, and Tuesday I went back to the doctor. We're trying a few medications."

"What changed? Is it because you're living on your own?" His tone softened. "Are you worried? Is it getting worse? What else aren't you telling me?"

He was tempted to let his brother believe that him moving out was the reason he'd gone back to the doctor, but he shook his head. "No, it's Hannah."

"What about her?"

"I'm in love with her."

Austin sat back, stunned. "And she talked sense into you and convinced you to go to the doctor?"

"Nooo." Randy gritted his teeth. "I thought if I could get it under control maybe I'd have a shot at a future with her. But I don't."

"What are you saying? You don't have long to live? Spill it all, Randy. How long do you have?"

He stared at the ceiling. He was botching this at every level. "I don't know, Austin. Could be years. Maybe I'll die an old man. Maybe not."

Austin nodded, his mouth thinning in a tight line.

"So she dumped you because of your heart. That's cold. I can't believe she would do that."

"NO! She would never do that." What was with this guy and jumping to conclusions? "I just realized I was kidding myself. Medications or not, this isn't going away."

They sat in silence for a few moments.

"I think you'd better tell me what you know about this heart thing." Austin's face had gone slack. "Why would the doctor put you on medications if they won't help prolong your life? Is there anything else you can do to protect yourself?"

"There's thickening in the ventricles, but I don't have the symptoms to require surgery. The meds are supposed to help slow down my heart rate and let the blood flow better. If they work, they'd reduce my chances of having a sudden heart attack."

"Well, why didn't you say so?" Austin's face cleared as he opened his hands and shook his head. "You're acting like you're going to fall over dead any minute, but these medications *can* save your life. Man, you're annoying."

"Then why aren't they working?" he snapped. "I've been light-headed, dizzy, tremors in my hands—you name it—for days. I don't want to live like that, feeling like I'm going to pass out all the time. I have no idea if I'm dealing with side effects of the medication or if I'm actually having a heart attack. No thanks."

"Go back to the doctor. Maybe there's a different drug without those side effects."

"Hannah called her brother. David stopped by the store after I passed out. He thinks the dosage is too high. He wants me to take half the doses of each until I can see my doctor."

Austin gave him a deadpan stare. "And you're just telling me this now?"

He shifted in his seat. "I hate the way I feel on them. I've managed this long without them."

"So what? You need the medication." Austin cocked his head, his jaw clenched. "I don't care if they made you feel a little woozy, you're not giving up on them. And you're not giving up on a future with Hannah, either. I never took you for a wimp, bro."

Randy stood and leaned over the island, pointing his finger in Austin's face. "Watch yourself."

He swiped the finger out of the way. "What's this really about?"

"You weren't there," he hissed. "When I found Dad. You have no idea what it was like."

"I saw." His eyes grew hard.

"But you didn't find him. You weren't the one who checked his cold neck to find a pulse. You didn't look into his lifeless eyes. You didn't find his dead body. I did!"

"I was there!" Austin slammed his fist down. "I lost him, too! If you don't think I wished a thousand times I could have spared you that, brother, then you don't know me. I hate that you found him. I would have done anything to shield you from that pain. But I didn't walk into his room that day. You did."

Everything hit Randy at once. His teeth chattered, his breathing grew shallow, and it was only the licking of his hand by Ned that brought him back to reality.

"Hey, I'm sorry," Austin said. "Are you okay?"

Randy nodded, and Austin came over and held him tightly.

Being in his brother's arms ripped the slightest of sobs

from him, and his shoulders began to shake as tears he'd held inside for over ten long years squeezed out.

He'd cried at Dad's funeral.

But he'd never dealt with the trauma of his sudden death.

He'd been holding in the fear of his own heart condition for so long that he hadn't realized what a burden it was to bear.

"It should have been me." Austin's words came out raspy. "I should have been the one to find him. I should be the one with the heart problem. I would take it from you, Randy. I would spare you... I don't want you to die. I love you. I can't lose you, too."

Hearing the words helped him pull himself together. He took a deep breath and stepped back.

"I never wanted you to find Dad. I just... I didn't want to find him, either. I wasn't ready. Wasn't prepared. And it *was* a shock. I couldn't process it."

"I couldn't, either." Austin raked his hand through his hair. "Now you know why I drank myself into a stupor in Texas that summer."

"Yeah."

They sat again, each lost in their thoughts. Ned had ambled to the mat near the patio door and lay with his chin on his paws.

"You really love Hannah, huh?" Austin angled his neck.

"I do." He slumped.

"Then what's really holding you back? Is this about your heart or Dad or what?"

For the first time, he didn't know. "My heart. I can't stop picturing her kneeling over my dead body. And I'm real torn on the issue of kids. You and I both know they'd have a fifty-fifty shot at inheriting this. What would it do to her? She's got so much love. You saw her with AJ. Knowing her own child had this heart condition would kill her."

"Maybe you're not giving her enough credit. I mean, what, you're going to be alone the rest of your life? To avoid having someone you love find your dead body?"

It didn't sound as rational coming from Austin.

"Someone *will* find your body someday, Randy. And, frankly, you could be the one to find her dead body. Would that make you want to avoid a relationship with her?"

The thought of finding Hannah the way he had his dad filled him with dread.

"You survived Dad's death." Austin gave him a pointed stare. "She'd survive finding you. You'd survive finding her." He checked his watch. "Listen, I've got to go. I told the babysitter I'd be back by eleven."

Randy followed him to the front door. Before leaving, Austin turned to him. "Stay on the meds for me, if not for yourself. I can't lose you."

With a lump in his throat, he nodded. Austin left, and he shut the door behind him.

*Is this about your heart or Dad or what?*

Randy climbed the stairs to his room. Ned followed him.

What was this about? He no longer knew, and what Austin had shared about wishing he'd been the one to find Dad, to spare him the pain? Randy had never really thought about how Austin felt back then. Hadn't realized his brother would feel guilty about not being the one to find their father.

It didn't surprise him. He should have known. Austin had always tried to shield him from pain.

Was that what he was trying to do with Hannah? Shield her from pain?

Or was he protecting himself?

Austin was right about everyone dying. And Hannah could very well die before him. Look at Joe and his wife, Linda. She'd fought cancer for a good chunk of their marriage.

Randy sat on the edge of the bed. If he stayed strong and ended things now, Hannah would slowly get over him and fall for someone else. Her worry about him would lessen in time. But could he live without her?

"What's wrong?" Mom rose from the couch as Hannah set her purse on an end table in their living room.

She'd texted Mom after the rehearsal dinner to tell her she was stopping by. Barley lifted his head from where he lay near Mom's feet, then he stood, stretched and wagged his tail all the way over to her.

Hannah petted him, comforted by his cheerful face. Then she looked up at her mother and couldn't keep it together anymore. "Everything's wrong."

Mom's expression softened. "Why don't you tell me about it?"

"Randy couldn't make it to the rehearsal. He wasn't feeling well." Sighing loudly, Hannah collapsed onto the couch.

"I'm sorry to hear that. David told us Ned was staying with Randy, but he didn't mention why."

"I really like him, Mom." Why was her throat constricting? She would *not* cry. "But I don't know if we have a future together."

"Oh?" Mom stared wide-eyed at her, waiting for her to continue.

"We had an argument. But it's more than disagreeing. It's...big, and I thought I could handle it, but now I don't know."

Mom's tender smile made the lump in her throat grow bigger.

"Honey, I don't know what it is, and I don't need to know. But I will tell you this. You have a big God who will be your strength when you're weak. So don't you worry about what you can handle and what you can't. God will always be by your side helping you through it."

For the first time in hours, a splash of hope lifted her spirits. "I don't know, Mom. I'm pretty intense. I always want everything to fall into place a certain way, you know? And I don't know if it will with him."

Mom just nodded.

"I want too much." Hannah picked at her sundress. "I worry too much. I think too much."

Admitting out loud what Shawn had said—what Randy had said—hurt, but it was also cathartic.

"Is that what you think?" She sounded surprised. "There's nothing wrong with feeling deeply. Caring deeply."

Wasn't there? "Maybe so, but it doesn't change anything."

"Well, honey, maybe Randy needs someone who thinks too much, worries too much, cares too much. You have a lot of energy. What's so bad about that?"

"You're just saying that because you're my mom."

"I'm saying it because it's true. You're special, Hannah. You pour your heart into everything you do, and that's becoming rarer these days. Don't look at your gifts as anything but good things."

Could her go-go personality be positive? When Shawn

had made it a negative? When even Randy teased her about it at times?

"I always thought I'd have a marriage like yours and Dad's." Her lips trembled, and she pressed them together to keep from crying. "I don't know what I want anymore."

Mom came over and sat beside her, putting her arm around her shoulders. "Pray about it. I don't know what this is all about, but I've always liked Randy. And I know he likes you. He's a good man. And he and Austin have done well for themselves being on their own for so long."

Hannah thought about having no parents or grandparents or extended family around. What would it have been like to lose both parents so young? She couldn't imagine.

"I guess it made them pretty independent." She glanced at her mother.

"It's hard to rely on someone else when you're used to relying on yourself."

She wouldn't argue with that. "Did you know Randy was the one who found his father the day he died?"

"I did." Mom scooched away a bit. "Always felt bad about it, too. Probably traumatized him for life."

"Yeah. I've always thought I have empathy, but I can't say I ever really put myself in his shoes."

"You do have empathy." Mom pointed to Barley, curled up near Hannah's feet. "Why else would you raise this puppy, knowing you have to give him up? I know you put yourself in Jenna's shoes because you've told me. And not just her, but Jackie's boy—little Damien—from last year. The boy who struggled with his reading. You were the one who worked with him after school. I could go on and on. You make a difference in people's lives. The same as Barley will someday."

"If he makes it into training." She gave her a wan smile.

"If I know you, he'll make it."

"Thanks, Mom."

"No matter what happens, I want you to know your dad and I couldn't be prouder of you. We love you exactly the way you are. Don't change a thing. Not for anyone. You're you for a reason."

"Well, don't make me cry," she teased, getting even more emotional.

"You want to stay here tonight?" Mom's eyes grew round with longing.

"No." She hated letting her down, but she needed to be alone. "I'm pretty tired. I'm going to take off. I'll text you when I get home."

A few minutes later, she hugged Mom goodbye and stepped out into the balmy night.

She was blessed to have a supportive mom and family. Randy only had Austin. And his friends, of course.

She wanted to be someone he could lean on, but he wanted to keep her at arm's length.

There was only so much she could do for someone who refused to include her in his life. And maybe she had to make peace with that.

## Chapter Thirteen

Randy lay awake in bed, staring at the ceiling. The clock showed 3:14 a.m. Ever since Austin left, he'd been combing through his memories, reviewing the past, thinking about the future. And he was no longer sure why he'd convinced himself he couldn't have a wife or kids. He wasn't sure about anything anymore.

Austin's confession about wishing he'd been the one to find Dad had toppled a tower of absolutes in his mind, revealing them to be lies.

*God, I was mad at You after Dad died. It didn't seem fair that I lost my mom as a little kid and then my dad. I loved him so much, and I didn't tell him. I didn't show him. I was such a stupid punk. Always thinking of myself, begging him to take me to another fishing tournament, whining about having to help with the ranch chores.*

Had he subconsciously thought he was being punished when he found his dad's body? For not loving ranch work the way Austin did? For being a pain in Dad's neck?

Randy swung his legs over the side of the bed. A few Bible passages had stuck in his mind over the years. *Trust in the Lord with all thine heart; and lean not unto thine own understanding. In all thy ways acknowledge Him, and He shall direct thy paths.*

He'd always lived the life of a Christian. But recently, his faith had gotten stronger. While he acknowledged his deep need for a Savior, he couldn't deny he'd been leaning on his own understanding. He hadn't allowed God to direct *all* his paths.

*What if You get it wrong, God? What if I trust You with my future, and it all falls apart?*

He cringed. What kind of faith assumed God would get it wrong?

*Lord, I want guarantees. About not dying, about Hannah, about kids. But that's not how You work. I'm scared. I'm scared to open my hands and give it all to You.*

Randy crossed over to the window. The stars shone bright against the black sky.

Austin was right. The medications prevented heart attacks. If he stayed on them, he would have a good shot at living for a long time. He'd have no reason to end things with Hannah.

*What about the kids?*

Could he do that to her? Could he subject her to the fear and anxiety?

Could he subject himself to it?

*She'd handle it fine. It's you who can't handle it.*

Hannah deserved to have a man who would cherish her, protect her, give her children, be strong for her.

*I'm not strong enough.*

The unwanted images from long ago marched through his mind and, no matter how hard he pushed, they wouldn't go away. His dad's lifeless body. The terror gripping him the instant he realized Dad was gone. The finality of it all.

And then he saw other images, ones he'd forgotten.

Of him and Austin standing by each other at the grave, their hands touching for the briefest of moments. Of them cleaning out Dad's room together in silence, fighting their emotions, doing what had to be done.

He could picture his father's smiling face, the pride in it, when he held up one of Randy's fishing trophies. He remembered his dad's arms around him and the hearty clap on his back with the words, "You did it, son."

Randy stared up at the moon, and the dread in his chest faded, replaced by something lighter, something more solid than the fear that had lived there for so many years.

All this time he'd thought he couldn't handle another loss. He'd handled the last one so poorly.

But he and Austin had gotten through it as best as they could.

He was older now. No longer a selfish teen.

Finding his father hadn't been a punishment. He might never know why he'd been the one to find Dad's body, but God had been with him and Austin through it all.

A wave of exhaustion hit him, and he crawled back into bed.

Everyone endured hard times. Maybe it was time for him to embrace the good times, too, instead of avoiding them out of fear.

Hannah hugged one knee to her chest. She'd tried sleeping, but after tossing and turning and trying to push away her thoughts, she'd given up. So here she was on the couch, sipping a cup of steaming hot Earl Grey tea with her thoughts buzzing around her mind like unruly kindergartners.

She missed her furry roommates—Ned, especially. It didn't matter that he liked Randy more than her. He was a comforting presence, an obedient dog, a help at all times. And he was a great role model for energetic Barley. That little butterball had wiggled his way into her heart the same way Ned had. The apartment felt quiet, lonely, empty without the dogs.

The same as her heart.

Lifting the mug to her lips, she barely tasted the tea. The dogs would be back on Sunday, but would they be enough? Or would her heart always be quiet, lonely and empty?

Sure, she missed them, but Randy was the one who'd filled that lonely spot inside her.

She hadn't been expecting it. Hadn't even noticed it happening, really. And now it was too late to do anything about it. If she would have heeded her own warnings last month, none of this would be happening.

She'd be training Barley and enjoying the summer without thinking about romance or marriage or children.

Her heart squeezed.

Why had she allowed herself to develop feelings for someone who'd closed himself off to all she had to offer?

Randy had nailed it earlier when he'd said she would worry about him. And if they had kids, she'd have to live with the daily anxiety of wondering if they inherited his heart condition.

Her personality had always been intense, even when it was in a good way. How many times had she been told she smiled too much? That she was too happy? What was she supposed to do? Frown all the time? Growl at people?

At every job she'd had, at least one coworker had com-

plained that she worked too hard. As if her giving it her
all was a bad thing.

Mom had made Hannah believe, for a second at least,
that her personality was a good thing.

But now? She wasn't so sure.

When she'd gotten home from her parents' house earlier, she'd taken pages of notes on Randy's condition.
Looked into every treatment. She'd been tempted to call
him or even text him to find out if he had any of the
symptoms listed besides the ones he'd told her about.

Randy was correct. Worrying about him went hand in
hand with loving him. She'd fuss over him. She'd probably smother him with her need to fix it—to fix him.

Maybe that was why he'd kept it from her. He didn't
want people weighing in on his personal life. And he
might be pushing her away because he feared she'd pressure him to change. His habits. His lifestyle.

If he decided not to take the medications—if he sim-
ply lived his life—would she be able to accept it? Or was
her love for him contingent on him doing what she felt
was necessary for him to stay healthy?

Setting the mug on the end table, she closed her eyes.
*God, I know Randy staying on his meds is the best course.
But what if he doesn't? It's not loving to just sit back and
watch someone make bad choices. If he stops treatment,
he could die.*

Even with treatment, he could die.

Abruptly, she stood. Why was she being so morbid?

*Because this is the reality of being with Randy. Not
knowing what the future holds. Not having any control.*

She sat on the couch again.

*That's the real issue, isn't it God? I want to be in
control.*

With her forehead in her hands, she tried to clear her head, but the thoughts kept coming, kept winding her up until her muscles roped into tight knots.

She wasn't in control. Not with Randy. Not with the dogs. Not with anything, really.

Randy had to make the choices that made sense to him, even if she didn't like them. They weren't hers to make.

*Okay, Lord, I want to do it Your way. You're going to have to show me how. I have no idea how to give up control with anything, let alone Randy's health.*

She slowly relaxed. Her mom's words from earlier came back. *Maybe Randy needs someone who thinks too much, cares too much, feels too much.*

Was Mom right?

The past month rushed back. Laughing with Randy, sitting on his beautiful back deck watching the world go by, talking about their childhood memories, relying on each other.

She didn't feel too intense when she was with him. In fact, he brought out her low-key side, and she hadn't even realized she had one of those.

*You're you for a reason.*

Randy was Randy for a reason, too. Heart condition and all.

Hannah squeezed her eyes shut and prayed. *Lord, we're two halves of a whole, aren't we? I need him, and he needs me. His disease is scary. I'm afraid he'll die. I'm scared he won't want kids, and I'm also scared that if he does want kids, they'll have the disease, too. I'm afraid he won't take his medication and will resent me for badgering him about it. A life with Randy would be filled with uncertainty. But Mom said You're strong when I'm weak, and I know it's true. I know it because it says so right in the Bible. And You've gotten me through tough times before.*

Her ex was correct. She was too much.

She curved her lips into a smile.

And she had too much love to throw away on someone who didn't recognize what a blessing she was.

Randy needed her. Now she just had to convince him to accept it.

## Chapter Fourteen

Randy woke with a start. Was he too late?

For what?

The wedding. Right. He sat up, stretched his arms over his head and went downstairs with Ned to start the coffee.

The sun was starting to rise. Looked like it was going to be a nice day for Sawyer to marry Tess.

"Did you sleep okay, boy? I'm sure glad you stayed with me last night." He bent down to give Ned a thorough petting. By the time he finished, the dog was positively smiling as his tongue lolled.

He filled the food bowl and gave him fresh water. Then he poured himself a cup of coffee and let the dog out on the deck with him. He held the mug in one hand as he leaned against the rail. A young deer, a doe from the looks of it, nibbled on weeds near the edge of the stream.

A deep sense of peace filled him.

The only thing missing was Hannah.

After last night, Randy no longer questioned his future. He wanted a full life, however long he had to live it.

He set the mug on the railing and padded back inside to find the two orange prescription bottles. He shook out one pill of each, took a knife out of the drawer along with a cutting board and cut each of them in half. Then he poured a glass of water and swallowed them before heading back out on the deck.

His future was too important to give up on the medicine. Hannah was worth any side effects. And so was he.

Ned trotted back up the steps and joined Randy. "God brought you and me together, Ned."

The dog had arrived in his life at the exact moment he'd needed him the most. All because of Hannah. She'd helped him out of a bind, given him hope. The same way her mother had years ago.

Miss Patty had reached out to him and Austin when they needed her the most after their dad died. And all these years, she'd been an emotional support to them, always letting them know she cared.

He'd taken her for granted, the same way he'd taken Ned's presence for granted, the same way he'd taken Hannah's generosity for granted. He'd wanted to repay her for all the wrong things.

Yes, she'd helped him run the store and volunteered to babysit AJ. She'd helped him paint and had found the nanny. All true.

But now what he really wanted to repay her for was her kindness, the way she'd opened her heart to him, the way she made him feel—accepted, important, cared for.

He didn't know what his future held, but he knew he wanted Hannah in it.

Lifting his mug again, he tried to figure out a plan. He'd give Joe a call later to pick up his truck. And then…

Should he wait until after the wedding to bare his heart? What if Hannah rejected him? What if she'd thought it through and realized that being with him was too much of a risk?

His brother had called him a wimp last night. His brother had been right.

No more playing it safe, hiding behind secrets.

He was going to talk to her this morning. Lay it all out there.

"Come on, bud. We've got a lot to do this morning if I'm going to win Hannah over."

Ned let out a woof.

"That's the spirit."

Should she take a chance and talk to Randy this morning? But what if he wouldn't listen to her? Then she'd be forced to go through the motions of the wedding with a fake smile on her face and a crushed heart.

Tomorrow would be better timing.

Hannah ran a comb through her damp hair and padded to the living room to click through the television channels. She stopped on a cooking show she typically enjoyed. She'd barely slept last night, but her entire body was keyed up with nervous energy. The wedding was still hours away.

Crossing over to the kitchen, she grabbed a banana off the counter and peeled it.

How was she going to convince him they were meant for each other?

If it wasn't for Ned, she might not have realized it. Sure, she and Randy had spent more time together because of Austin and the baby, but Ned had been the key to them getting closer over the past couple of weeks.

Not only did the sweet dog play accidental matchmaker, but he also had the potential to save Randy's life. Ned already alerted him whenever he had symptoms. Every moment counted when dealing with a potential heart attack.

She took another bite of banana. She'd train five dogs if it meant Randy's life would be prolonged for even one day. And she planned on being right there by his side.

If she could get through to him…

Mom was right—she was who she was—so if Randy was going to be with her, he'd have to understand that a certain amount of prodding regarding his health would come with the territory. He might call it fussing. She called it caring.

And they'd have to navigate the issue of kids together. If she could handle the man she loved having a heart condition, chances were, she could handle her children being diagnosed, too. If their kids had it, they wouldn't be able to take part in high-activity sports, but that was a small price to pay to live.

She kept eating the banana, but doubts crept in. Would Randy listen to her? Or was he so stuck in his ways that he'd refuse to consider a relationship with her?

*God, please open his heart to what I have to say.*

Chucking the banana peel into the trash, she headed to her bedroom. Forget waiting until after the wedding. It would be torture. She had to talk to him this morning.

She picked out a pale pink sundress, applied a little makeup and blow-dried her hair.

No matter what, she was insisting Randy keep Ned. It was a hard sacrifice to make. She loved the black Lab even though he preferred Randy's company. But Randy's life might depend on the dog, and it would be wrong to deny Ned a chance to use his hard-earned skills with the man he'd bonded with. The two belonged together.

She just hoped Randy would see that she belonged with him, too.

\* \* \*

Randy stood outside Hannah's apartment door with Ned by his side and pulled back his shoulders. He'd stopped by the candy store and bought their largest box of homemade chocolates. Then he'd stopped by the flower shop and bought a huge bouquet of yellow roses. If the jeweler had been open, he would have picked out a ring.

Everyone in town would surely be gossiping about these purchases by noon. *Let them.*

He was ready to wear his heart on his sleeve when it came to the most beautiful girl in the world—pure sunshine, his Hannah.

He glanced down at the dog. Ned looked up at him and thumped his tail as if to say, *What are you waiting for? Let me in!*

Randy closed his eyes briefly. *God, I don't know what I'm going to say to her. Will You help me?* Then he knocked. The door opened instantly, and he stared into Hannah's impossibly blue eyes, noting the way her mouth formed an O.

"Do you have a minute?" he asked.

She nodded. Her blond hair fell in waves and she wore a pretty pink dress. Man, would he like to hold her in his arms right now.

Ned had already surged inside and rubbed against her skirt. She laughed and petted him, bending to scratch behind his ears and talking to him in what Randy considered her dog-talk voice, which was just as goofy but lower than the baby-talk voice she used with AJ.

"Are those for me?" She straightened, pointing to the roses in his hand. Dumbstruck, he nodded. He handed her the flowers and the chocolates, then followed her to the kitchen, where she busied herself by putting the roses in a vase. When she finished arranging them, she gestured to the living area.

He took a seat on the couch with his knees wide and elbows propped on them. His right leg seemed to have a life of its own as the knee bounced rapidly. Every time he stopped it, it started again.

How to start this conversation? He didn't know where to begin.

"Are you feeling okay?" she asked, smoothing the skirt over her legs in the chair opposite him.

"Yep." His tongue might as well be six inches thick. "You?"

She nodded.

*Get it together!*

"I've been thinking about what you said yesterday." There. Something intelligent had finally come out of his mouth. "About me making all the rules. You're right. And it's not fair."

She looked like she wanted to say something, but when she didn't, he plowed forward.

"I made a lot of rules for myself after Dad died and I got my diagnosis. I didn't know it at the time, but I decided playing it safe and hiding my condition from everyone was in my best interests. Now, don't get me wrong, I don't plan on announcing my condition in the church bulletin anytime soon, but I should have told Austin."

"Did you tell him?"

"Last night." His heart began to thump just thinking about it. Ned got up and sat next to him. He chuckled. "See? Ned knows it was a tough conversation."

A hint of a smile played on her lips.

"We're good now. But I didn't get much sleep last

night. I felt bad—torn about you and me. And I didn't see a way through. I love you, and I don't want to hurt you."

"I know you don't," she said quietly, her eyes losing their shimmer.

"But I also don't want to be a coward, and that's what I've been. I've been protecting my emotions, hiding behind my heart. Ironic, isn't it? You have my heart, but because of the disease, I wouldn't let you claim it." He was rambling. Putting off the substance in case she didn't like it. "I followed your brother's advice today. I cut the dosage in half."

There was the smile he knew and loved. "Have you noticed a difference? Is it making you dizzy?"

"That's not the point." His knee was still bouncing. Ned licked his hand. "The point is I'm going to do everything I can to live a long life. The medications are supposed to prevent me from having a sudden heart attack. I don't know if they will, but I'm willing to try them."

"Oh, Randy, I'm glad." Her eyes grew misty. "I've been so worried about you."

Seeing her concern brought an uncomfortable feeling to his gut. *Get used to it. You're going to have to let her worry about you if you two are going to be together.*

Her chin lifted. "I'm going to do everything I can to prevent you from having a sudden heart attack, too."

He didn't like the sound of that. What was she talking about?

"I want you to have Ned."

Ned? He stared at her, not comprehending. "Come again?"

"Ned." She nodded, pointing to the dog, who sat on the floor next to him. "You two belong together. He's trained to help you. He clearly wants to be with you. It gives him a chance to do the work he loves. He'll alert you whenever you're having symptoms, and it might give you enough of a warning to call 911 if things get bad."

She was giving him her dog? The one she'd waited over a year to adopt? The one he knew she loved?

Why? Why would she do that?

Unless…was this her way of rejecting him?

He needed to clear the air immediately.

"Hannah, I was wrong yesterday. I shouldn't have pushed you away. I love you. And I…I want to be with you. But if you've thought it over and realize my health is too much for you—that this whole situation is too much—I understand. You don't have to give me your dog."

Hannah gaped at him. Did Randy just say his heart condition was too much for her? That he was too much?

A laugh burst from her mouth—a hysterical, strangled laugh. She clamped her hand over her lips, but it continued.

"What? I didn't say anything funny." He stiffened.

"I know you didn't." She forced herself to calm down. Of all the things he could have said to her, she never would have guessed he'd say that. "No, Randy, you're not too much. Your heart condition isn't too much. I laughed because my ex-boyfriend broke up with me, claiming I was too much. So to hear you—someone who has a knack for making people feel comfortable—claim you might be too much? Well, it's absurd."

He looked at her as if she'd grown a third eye. Maybe she had.

"I'm the one who's too much, Randy." She leaned forward and pointed to her chest. "Me. You were right all along. I think too much. I worry too much. And that's not going to change. But you know what else? I care too much, and I help too much, and I love too much. That's the way God made me."

"You're not too much, Hannah. You're everything I've ever wanted."

She held those words close to her heart.

"Look," he said. "I don't know how much time I have on this earth, and I know it isn't fair to ask you to spend that time with me. But, Hannah, I love you. I know you're going to fuss over me. I know you're going to fuss over our kids someday. I want you to, because it's a blessing to have someone care enough to fuss over you. I promise I'll listen to you. I'll do whatever it takes to make you happy, because you make me happy."

She didn't realize she'd been holding her breath until it blew out in a whoosh. Randy got up and walked over to her, holding out his hand. She placed hers in his and allowed him to help her to her feet.

He looked down at her with such tenderness and fire it was all she could do to stay standing. Then his hands wrapped around her lower back.

"I've known you my whole life, but I never knew a girl like you existed. I was blind." His voice grew husky. "You give and give and give—and you act like it's nothing. You're always smiling. Always making me feel light and good and like life's worth living."

She almost swooned. But she had things to say, too, and she needed to get them out.

"I know why you tried to push me away, Randy, and I'm not mad about it." She placed her palms against his chest. His strong, muscular chest. "I understand. You kept your health problems private to protect me and your brother from pain. I'm glad you've moved past that. Loving someone doesn't mean hiding the hard stuff. It means sharing the hard stuff. Getting through it together."

He tightened his hold on her waist, and she wound her arms around his neck.

"We're good together," she said. "I don't know if I've told you how much I admire what you've done with your life—the store, the house. You're not afraid to go after what you want. I like being with you. You mellow me out. You help me unwind. I feel like a different part of me comes out when I'm with you. That probably doesn't make sense. Anyway, I will try very hard not to nag you about your heart if you'll trust me with your symptoms and treatment options. I'm aware this is something I'm going to have to trust God with, and I won't always succeed."

"I feel alive and free when I'm with you, Hannah. I like how you don't take things too seriously—how you tease me. I like that you've dedicated your life to teaching kids. I like that you're willing to give your time, your money and your heart to raise a puppy who will be a service dog. As for my health, we'll both have to trust God with it."

His gaze trapped hers, and if she had any doubts, the sincerity in his eyes chased them away.

He lowered his mouth and kissed her. She pressed closer, tasting so much promise in his kiss. How she loved this man. She'd do anything for him. His strength enveloped her, his hands caressing her bare arms, and she shivered, knowing he loved her as much as she did him.

When they broke away, he tenderly touched her hair, smiling at her.

"What a summer, huh?" she said. "I adopted a dog, ran a tackle shop for a week, cared for a baby for another week, brought a puppy home and fell in love. And summer's only just begun."

"I know, right?"

"What do you think the rest of the summer will bring?"

He grinned. "I'm hoping it will bring a ring on your finger and a date for us to get married. My big house is lonely without you."

She loved the sound of that. Her heart was so full it was ready to burst.

"First we need to get through today's wedding." She burrowed into his arms, glancing up at him. "I'll need to get ready."

"It's hours away. Let's have breakfast first." But he didn't move toward the kitchen. Instead, he kissed her again.

"Breakfast is overrated." And she kissed him back.

## Chapter Fifteen

The six friends gathered in a corner under the big tent on Tess and Sawyer's ranch that evening. Randy waited for them to stop gabbing. The wedding ceremony had been touching, if hot. Sunrise Bend was scorching for early July. Tess's father, Ken McCay, had wiped tears from his eyes after giving her away. It had been nice to see him feeling better after his cancer treatments over the winter. And now the reception was about to begin. But first…

Randy glanced at his best friends, all decked out in tuxes, and knew the time was right.

He was telling them about his heart condition. And he was telling them about Hannah. Right now.

"Before we get to celebrating, I have a couple of things to tell you." Randy got their attention, and they moved closer, forming a circle. "I couldn't be here yesterday because I passed out. I have a heart condition—the same one as my father—and I've been ignoring it for years."

"What happened?" Blaine looked concerned.

"I'm on medications, and they made me light-headed. I'm going to work with my doctor to get them balanced so they can do their job."

"How life-threatening is this?" Mac asked.

Randy shrugged. "If the meds do what they're supposed to, I should be okay. There's no cure."

The other guys asked a few questions, and he answered them as best he could. Then he took a deep breath.

"The other thing I want to tell you is Hannah and I are dating."

A collective *whoop* filled the air.

Their knowing grins had him shaking his head.

"What happened to *I'm never getting married or having kids*?" Blaine acted disgusted. "That changed quick."

"When a good woman comes along…" Randy grinned. "By the way, you know Ned is a former service dog, right?" They nodded. "Well, he's really good at alerting me whenever I'm having symptoms related to my blood pressure and heart."

"Oh, I see," Jet teased. "You get the girl and the dog. It's a two-for-one."

They all laughed.

Mac's phone rang, and he answered it. They joked around for a minute, but they all quieted when they saw the blood drain from his face. He hung up the phone, his eyes somewhere far away, somewhere bleak.

"That was the police department in Celina. Dad and Jeanette took off for Vegas on his two-seater plane earlier. It crashed. They didn't make it." His knuckles grew white from gripping the cell phone.

Austin sprang into action, taking the phone from Mac's hand and putting his arm around his shoulders.

Sawyer looked shell-shocked. "I'm sorry, Mac. I can't believe it."

Mac's eyes darted back and forth, not really seeing anything.

"Did they say anything about Kaylee?" Jet asked.

The words snapped Mac out of his stupor. "She wasn't with them. She's staying at a friend's house this weekend. I have to go. I have to get down to Texas."

Randy and Blaine exchanged glances. "You need us to drive you to the airport?"

"No. I'll have Otis take me." Mac's color returned. Otis was his ranch manager. "You guys enjoy the reception. Sawyer, I hate to bail on you like this—"

"You're not. Go." Sawyer shook his head. "And if you need anything, we're here for you."

Mac gave him a grim nod, then left.

The five of them stood there, staring at each other, stunned at what had just happened. Tess headed their way, her wedding gown swishing around her and a huge smile on her face. As she neared, she slowed, the smile fading.

"What's wrong?" she asked. The bridesmaids—Erica, Reagan, Hannah, Holly and Bridget, who was Sawyer's friend, followed behind her in pale purple dresses. Randy only had eyes for Hannah. Sawyer waited until they all gathered.

"Mac's dad and stepmom were in an accident. He had to leave."

"Are they going to be okay?" Erica asked.

Sawyer clenched his jaw and gave a quick shake of his head.

Gasps of horror filled the air. Randy went to Hannah and slipped his arm around her waist, kissing her temple. "Are you okay?"

She looked up at him through anguished eyes and nodded. "Poor Mac."

Austin raised his hands. "He's going to Texas tonight.

In the meantime, we're celebrating this wedding. There's a time to mourn and a time to rejoice, and this—right here, right now—is a time to rejoice. If any of you need some support, you can talk to the pastor. I'll go fill him in."

Randy met Austin's gaze and nodded. His brother was good at taking charge and dealing with tough situations. He wished he had trusted Austin with his health sooner. He would have handled it just fine. At least they all knew the truth about his heart now.

He squeezed Hannah's hand.

Tonight, they'd celebrate. Tomorrow, they'd mourn.

"Come on, let's tell my parents we're dating." After the meal had been served and the cake had been cut, Hannah led Randy to the center of the tent, where her parents, brothers, sisters-in-law and the kiddos were sitting at a table.

"You haven't told them?" His eyes twinkled as he pretended to be shocked.

"Very funny. I haven't had time. I did fill the girls in earlier. They're *very* happy for us."

He stayed close by her side. "How do you think your dad will react?"

She pulled a face and shrugged. "Michael threatened my prom date with unspeakable torture if I wasn't home by midnight. You might want to worry about his reaction more than Dad's."

"That isn't reassuring."

They weaved around the tables, stopping to chat with friends along the way. Finally, they made it to the table. Hannah's pulse was racing as she took in the chaos— Leann had both her toddler son, Cam, and Tess's toddler son, Tucker, on her lap. How she managed to keep both energetic boys there, Hannah couldn't say. Kelli, meanwhile, was pointing Rachel and Sunni in the general direction of the cake, while Mom held little Owen on her lap. Dad and Michael laughed at something, and David had turned away to talk to someone else.

"Okay, everyone." Hannah waited until she had their attention, "I'm going to make this short and sweet. Randy and I are dating. More than dating, really. We're—well, I love him."

Mom set Owen on Michael's lap and rushed to Randy with open arms. "Oh, honey, that's the best news."

Hannah's jaw dropped to the floor as her mom hugged Randy before her. "Um, hello? What about me?"

Mom shifted to hug her, laughing and grinning. "I knew you were right for each other. Haven't I been saying you need to date one of the nice cowboys around here?"

"He's technically not a cowboy." Hannah tilted her head.

"He was raised on a ranch." Mom's tone wasn't to be argued with. She leaned in so only Hannah could hear. "He's the one, Hannah. You've got yourself a good man."

"Thanks, Mom." They exchanged a glance full of understanding. Then Leann and Kelli were hugging her, while Michael and David stood to badger Randy and clap him on the back.

Hannah tried to hear what they were saying, but the noise level was through the roof. The next thing she knew, Randy was getting dragged by little Rachel to the dance floor. He caught Hannah's eyes and grinned. She waved to him, laughing as her niece chattered the entire way. He'd get used to being part of a big, loud family. Eventually.

Dad stood in front of her with a stern expression. "Does he treat you right?"

"He does." She suddenly felt like a ten-year-old.

"He'd better. If he doesn't, he'll have me and your brothers to contend with." Dad locked his fingers together and cracked his knuckles. She gulped. "Don't look so scared." He smiled. "I've always liked Randy. He's good for you."

She threw her arms around her father. "I love you, Dad."

"I love you, too, Hannah Banana."

She chatted with her family until the crowd shifted and she spotted Cassie holding AJ. She went over to them.

"How is this little cutiebug?" Hannah took him from Cassie, and he gripped a teething ring in one hand and cooed to her. His plump body felt a little heavier than it had the last time she'd held him. "Oh, you're growing up too fast."

"He's doing good, isn't he?" Cassie's face was full of affection for the boy. "Thank you, again, for telling me about the nanny position. It's working out great. I can help Mom with Gramps in the evening and take care of AJ during the day."

"God worked it out. Austin needed you desperately. We all did, really."

Cassie laughed. "Well, I needed the job desperately."

They caught up a few more minutes before Hannah kissed the top of the baby's head and handed him back to her.

"Come here." Randy took her hand. She hadn't seen him come up behind her. She gave him a smile and allowed him to lead her to the dance floor.

"Where are we going?"

"They're playing our song."

"Our song is *not* 'All My Exes Live in Texas.' Really, Randy?" She halted.

"Not this song. The next one." He held her hand firmly and tugged.

"It had better be good."

"It will be." He grinned as he pulled her onto the dance floor and into his arms. As if on cue, "When You Say Nothing At All" began to play. "See?"

Her heart filled with love for this man. She reached up and gave him a light kiss. "I stand corrected. I love you."

"I love you, too." He dropped his forehead to hers. "You have my heart."

"Ned and I will keep it beating. Don't you worry."

He laughed. "You'd better. Now that you're mine, I have a lot of plans for us."

"Oh yeah? Like what?"

"Like fishing up in Montana in a few weeks. I know the best spot..."

"Such a romantic." Her deadpan tone made him chuckle. "I have plans, too."

"Name it and I'm in."

"You don't even know what I want to do."

"If you're there, I am, too." And she could tell he meant it.

"In that case..." She laughed as he spun her in a circle.

"Life's better with you, Hannah."

She'd never tire of hearing those words.

# Epilogue

"Wake up!" Randy bellowed into Austin's ear. "I've got to take off." It was Saturday morning of Labor Day weekend, and he was kicking it off right.

"What? What's going on?" Austin jolted up in bed, rubbing his eyes. "Is it AJ?"

"No, he's sleeping. I need the good platter. The one that matches Mom's dishes. You know, the one with the roses. Where'd you put it?"

Today was the day Randy was proposing to Hannah. After a summer of training Barley, who was turning into a good-natured, disciplined dog, hanging out on weeknights, driving her to his favorite fishing spots and having Sunday suppers with her big family, Randy was ready to make it official.

He wanted Hannah to be his wife more than anything in the world.

"If I don't hurry, I won't be able to surprise her." Not that she was going anywhere this early on a Saturday.

"I thought you were waiting until tonight." Austin got out of bed. "What changed?"

"I can't wait that long. I'm bringing breakfast over and popping the question."

"You're not seriously tying the ring to the end of a fishing pole and pretending to reel her in, are you?" Austin's arm grazed his as he left the room. Randy was at his heels.

"No." He couldn't keep the hurt out of his tone. He'd always thought the ring on the fishing pole was perfect for proposing. But he had a better plan now. "Mac's genius idea of me tossing the ring box in her lap and saying, 'Well?' was worse."

"Yeah, I'm worried about him. He hasn't been himself since his dad died."

"Raising Kaylee can't be easy, either."

"Well, she *is* fifteen. It's not like bringing home a baby." They met each other's eyes and laughed. "Remember the first time you tried to change AJ's diaper?"

"I'll never forget it." Randy shook his head, enjoying the memory. "Sorry, man, I think I threw away half the kid's wardrobe. I couldn't stand dealing with those blowout diapers."

"Between you and me, I threw away the other half. I couldn't, either."

They went into the dining room, where the hutch filled with the good dishes was located.

"The platter, you said?" Austin poked around the upper shelf. "I thought it was up here. Oh, wait. I moved it down below." He crouched, opening the doors at the bottom. He rooted through the clutter until he found it. He took out the platter and handed it to Randy.

As soon as it was in his hands, he got jittery. Ned joined them, watching him. "It's okay, buddy. This is a good heartbeat thing."

"Need anything else?" Austin asked.

"Nope. I'll call you later to let you know how it goes."

Austin gave him a quick hug. "Don't worry. She'll say yes."

He gulped, nodding, and snapped his fingers for Ned to come. Minutes later, he was driving back to town. He'd showered earlier and changed into a crisp button-down shirt and his best jeans. The ring box was in his pocket. All he had to do was stop at the Barking Squirrel to pick up the breakfast for two he'd ordered and take it to Hannah's.

Twenty minutes later, he parked near her apartment. With trembling fingers, he took out the jewelry box. Opening it, he stared at the round diamond with the twisted halo of diamonds surrounding it. He'd instantly known it was the one. Just like he knew Hannah was the one.

He tied a pink ribbon around it, then attached it to Ned's collar and tucked it under so she wouldn't see it right away. Then he gathered the box holding two place settings of his mom's dishes, hooked the bag of food over his wrist and got out of the truck. Ned joined him, and his palms grew clammy and his heartbeat thumped as he knocked on the door, waiting for her to answer.

The door flung open, and Hannah's smiling face chased away all his fears. Barley stood next to her, and Ned walked inside, greeting Barley and going down the hall.

"Here, let me take something." She wore a pair of jeans that fit just right with a pretty, short-sleeved shirt.

"No, I've got it." He went straight to the kitchen and set everything down on the counter. Then he dished the food onto his mother's plates.

"Wow, this is fancy." She brought two mugs of coffee

over to the table where he was setting the plates. "Ooh, is that cinnamon French toast?"

"I know you have a thing for it." He knew her favorite foods. He'd memorized them all.

There was no way he'd be able to eat a bite of this delicious meal until he asked her the important question—the big one. He gulped.

She reached for a chair, but he placed his hand over hers. She frowned, meeting his eyes.

"Wait." He swallowed. "Before we eat, there's something I need to say."

She looked even more confused.

"I love you."

"I love you, too." She smiled.

"Every day that goes by I'm more convinced we belong together." The side effects of the medications had all but disappeared since the doctor adjusted his doses, and he felt better about the future, whether he died suddenly or not. He and Hannah had also talked on several occasions about getting married and having children and what that would entail.

Life was full of risks, and it was a risk they were both willing to take, even if one or more of their kids ended up inheriting his condition.

"I am, too."

"Good. Because I'm ready for more. You're the sunshine in my life. You brought hope to me. You're pretty as any flower I've ever seen, and you're sweeter than sugar. I know that sounds corny, but it's true. That house of mine feels awfully lonely whenever you aren't in it. I'm ready to change that if you are." He got down on one knee. "Hannah Carr, will you marry me?"

"Yes!" She threw her arms around his neck, and he

lifted her off her feet. Then he slowly set her back down, keeping her close to him, and kissed her. Thoroughly.

This woman. He'd walk through fire for her. Take a bullet for her. Go shopping all day at a mall for her. He loved her that much.

"I love your enthusiasm," he said, his voice husky. "I love the way you go after the things you want. I love your patience when you're working with Barley. I love the way your hair curls when it's rainy. I love that I'm the one you ask to take the top panels off the Jeep on nice days. I love your smile. And I love your mom's brownies."

"Everyone loves Mom's brownies."

"I think she puts extra love in mine or something."

"I wouldn't put it past her." She grinned, then bit her lower lip. "Um, Randy?"

"Yeah?"

"I don't mean to sound whiny or anything, but is there a ring?"

He stepped back, smacking his forehead. He'd forgotten the most important part!

"Ned," he called. The Lab wagged his tail all the way over, and Randy almost laughed as he saw that the pink ribbon had come loose from where he'd tucked it, leaving the ring dangling near his doggy chest. "I had a whole speech planned and everything. How the dog knew my heart better than I did, and it was only fair to have him give you mine."

She spotted the ring instantly and hugged Ned, who licked her face before she untied the ribbon. Randy helped slide it on her finger. She beamed up at him, her eyes glistening. "It's perfect."

"Well, shall we set the date?"

Her laugh rang out loudly. "When you're ready for something, you don't wait around, do you?"

"Not when I see what I like. And I like you."

"My knees are going to buckle if you keep talking like that."

"I'll be here to catch you if they do."

\* \* \* \* \*

*If you enjoyed this K-9 Companions book, be sure to look for* An Unlikely Alliance *by Toni Shiloh, available July 2022 wherever Love Inspired books are sold!*

*And don't miss the previous books in Jill Kemerer's Wyoming Ranchers miniseries:*

The Prodigal's Holiday Hope
A Cowboy to Rely On

*Available now from Love Inspired!*

Dear Reader,

From the moment I introduced readers to Hannah and Randy in the novella *A Merry Wyoming Christmas*, I knew I had to write their story. Hannah is such an energetic, generous, fun woman—the kind of friend I love to have in real life! She needed a man who would appreciate all she brings to a relationship, and Randy didn't know it at first, but he was that man.

Secrets have a way of isolating us from the people we love. Randy's decision not to tell anyone about his chronic health problem is common. It's natural to want to protect our loved ones from pain and from worry. But by doing so, Randy was shortchanging his brother and Hannah. When he did confide in them, they helped lighten his burdens. God is good at putting people in our lives when we need them the most.

And Ned! Oh, how I love that dog. I'm so glad he found a home where he could use his gifts to help Randy, and I applaud Hannah for unselfishly allowing him to be with Randy when she wanted to bond with the dog herself. Service dogs are incredible, wonderful animals. I'm thankful for everyone who helps train them.

I hope you enjoyed this book. I love connecting with readers. Feel free to email me at jill@jillkemerer.com or write me at PO Box 2802, Whitehouse, Ohio, 43571.

God bless you,
*Jill Kemerer*

# LOVE INSPIRED

*Stories to uplift and inspire*

---

Fall in love with Love Inspired—
inspirational and uplifting stories of faith
and hope. Find strength and comfort in
the bonds of friendship and community.
Revel in the warmth of possibility and the
promise of new beginnings.

Sign up for the Love Inspired newsletter
at **LoveInspired.com** to be the first
to find out about upcoming titles,
special promotions and exclusive content.

---

## CONNECT WITH US AT:

 Facebook.com/LoveInspiredBooks

Twitter.com/LoveInspiredBks

LISOCIAL2021

# COMING NEXT MONTH FROM
## Love Inspired

## HER FORBIDDEN AMISH CHILD
*Secret Amish Babies* • by Leigh Bale
Four years after bearing a child out of wedlock, Tessa Miller is determined to provide for her son—even if it means working at the diner run by her ex-fiancé, Caleb Yoder. Yet revealing the truth about her past could be the key to the reunion she's never stopped wanting...

## FINDING HER AMISH HOME
by Pamela Desmond Wright
After her sister's death, Maddie Baum flees to Wisconsin Amish country with her nephew to protect him from his criminal father. But can she keep the secret from handsome Amish shopkeeper Abram Mueller, who might be the chance at happiness she's been waiting for?

## AN UNLIKELY ALLIANCE
*K-9 Companions* • by Toni Shiloh
With her emotional support dog at her side, Jalissa Tucker will do whatever it takes to ensure the survival of the local animal rescue—even ally herself with her nemesis, firefighter Jeremy Rider. As working together dredges up old hurts, putting the past aside could be the key to their future joy...

## A PLACE TO HEAL
by Allie Pleiter
Opening a camp for children who've dealt with tragedy is former police detective Dana Preston's goal in life. And she's found the perfect location—Mason Avery's land. But convincing the widowed dad—and the town—to agree might take a little prayer and a lot of hard work...

## THE SOLDIER'S BABY PROMISE
by Gabrielle Meyer
Resolved to keep his promise, Lieutenant Nate Marshall returns to Timber Falls to look after his first love—and the widow of his best friend, who was killed in action. Grieving mom Adley Wilson is overwhelmed by her bee farm and her new baby, and accepting Nate's help may just be the lifeline she needs...

## THE TWINS' ALASKAN ADVENTURE
*Home to Hearts Bay* • by Heidi McCahan
When Tate Adams returns to Hearts Bay, Alaska, for the summer with his adorable twins in tow, Eliana Madden is determined not to fall in love with him again. But she can't refuse when he asks for her help caring for his preschoolers. Could this be the start of a new adventure for them all?

---

**LOOK FOR THESE AND OTHER LOVE INSPIRED BOOKS WHEREVER BOOKS ARE SOLD, INCLUDING MOST BOOKSTORES, SUPERMARKETS, DISCOUNT STORES AND DRUGSTORES.**

LICNM0522

# Get 4 FREE REWARDS!

## We'll send you 2 FREE Books plus 2 FREE Mystery Gifts.